Also by William Sleator

Novels

Blackbriar
House of Stairs
Into the Dream
The Green Futures of Tycho
Run
Fingers
Interstellar Pig
Singularity
The Boy Who Reversed Himself
The Duplicate
Strange Attractors
The Spirit House
Others See Us
Dangerous Wishes
The Night the Heads Came
The Beasties
The Boxes
Rewind
Boltzmon!
Marco's Millions
Parasite Pig
The Boy Who Couldn't Die
The Last Universe
Hell Phone

Books for Younger Readers

The Angry Moon
Among the Dolls
Once, Said Darlene
That's Silly

Short Story Collection

Oddballs

WITHDRAWN

WILLIAM SLEATOR

Amulet Books
New York

Library of Congress Cataloging-in-Publication Data

Sleator, William.
Test / by William Sleator.
p. cm.
Summary: In the security-obsessed, elitist United States of the near future, where a standardized test determines each person's entire future, a powerful man runs a corrupt empire until seventeen-year-old Ann and other students take the lead in boycotting the test.
ISBN-13: 978-0-8109-9356-3
ISBN-10: 0-8109-9356-2
[1. Educational tests and measurements—Fiction.
2. Education—Fiction. 3. Political corruption—Fiction.
4. Immigrants—Fiction. 5. Conspiracies—Fiction.] I. Title.

PZ7.S6313Tes 2008
[Fic]—dc22
2007038987

Text copyright © 2008 William Sleator
Book design by Chad W. Beckerman

Printed and bound in U.S.A.
10 9 8 7 6 5 4 3 2 1

HNA ▮▮▮▮▮
harry n. abrams, inc.
a subsidiary of La Martinière Groupe

115 West 18th Street
New York, NY 10011
www.hnabooks.com

For Ann Monticone,

who is really the co-author of this book,

a wonderful teacher, and my best friend.

Not everything that can be
counted counts, and not
everything that counts
can be counted.
—Albert Einstein

The first time the black motorcycle followed Ann on her way to school was a Wednesday in early May.

She noticed it immediately because of the red logo on the front fender, and also on the driver's helmet. It was a striking logo, and she knew she had seen it somewhere before, though she couldn't remember where. But the logo made it easy for her to be sure it was the same black motorcycle she had seen—also just behind her—a block or so before, and another time before that. That logo, and the very expensive silver-studded black leather jacket the driver wore.

The red logo was egg-shaped, made up of three reptilian curvy creatures swirling around each other forming the egg. She didn't like it, and she felt afraid that the motorcycle really did seem to be following her.

She brooded about it in school all day. She was able to hide her preoccupation at lunch with her friends, but not in Mr. Wells's English class in the afternoon. Wells, who always seemed to be dressed in gray, and always had a handkerchief to wipe the sweat off his forehead, noticed that she was preoccupied, even as he was ranting at the class about the upcoming XCAS test, and how low their practice test scores were. He stopped pacing and turned on her. "You'd better concentrate on what I'm saying, young lady," he said to her. "Or haven't you noticed that your test prep scores have been going down?"

The entire class turned and looked at her, which made her angry and embarrassed. The strange foreign boy, Lep, was the only one who had a sympathetic look on his face.

Wells caught that too. "Don't waste your time feeling sorry for her, Fingernail," Wells taunted him.

At the beginning of the year Wells had made him explain that his nickname, Lep, meant "fingernail" in whatever language they spoke in the country he came from, and Wells used it to make fun of him when he was in a bad mood. "You may think you're doing better, but you're not nearly good enough yet to pass XCAS yourself."

Lep looked down at his desk.

Ann was nervous about the motorcycle on her way home from school. She always walked to and from school, even after she'd been hanging out with her friends. Walking was just so much faster than taking the bus, or riding in somebody's car. Because of the traffic, of course. The traffic that was always there, except for at three A.M. The traffic that oozed along agonizingly, inch by sluggish, groaning inch. The traffic that sat forever at red lights too far away to be seen. And then moved slowly forward. And then stopped again, many times, before it even reached the light.

She'd been walking home from school for the last few years, and yet she still never failed to appreciate how lucky she was that she lived close enough to be *able* to walk, instead of being trapped in a car like so many of the other kids. Yes, on good days it took her just over an hour, and on bad days in the winter even longer. But that was still so much better than the four or even more hours other kids had to suffer through in cramped vehicles, trying to do their homework and study for the XCAS test and getting carsick.

She knew what it was like. Until a few years ago she had been relegated to the school buses herself, because of the gangs on the street. Walking hadn't been safe. But that was before the new government took over, with their heightened security. Of course there had always been security at school. Now all the cars had to go through security checkpoints too, at regular intervals, which slowed things down even more.

But she was free. She had to wear a mask, of course; everybody did in the pollution. But she could go at her own pace; she wasn't under the total control of the traffic like people in buses and cars. She could even jog when she felt like it, though actually running would have been too suspicious. She was seventeen, after all, and not a little girl anymore.

She checked behind her and there was that motorcycle again, with the red reptilian logo. It was closer behind her than it had been on her way to school. It had been very odd before. Now it was scary.

Logos were everywhere, of course, representing every company, blurring together indiscriminately. And yet somehow this one stood out. She thought she had seen it only one other place before now. But where?

She quickly turned away from the motorcycle and started walking faster. She wanted to get home! She looked at her watch. At least another half hour to go.

If it had been a car it wouldn't have been able to follow her; it would have been stuck in traffic and she would have zipped past it ages ago. But motorcycles had more mobility; they could weave in and out between the trapped cars. Motorcycles always thrummed at the head of the cars at every traffic light. The instant the light turned green they were the first ones to zoom roaring ahead in clouds of exhaust. Only because it was a motorcycle was it able to follow her.

But how could she be so sure it was really following her? Maybe she was just being paranoid. She turned back and looked again to check.

And when she did, the driver—whose face was completely hidden by the dark helmet with the red reptilian logo on it—made the unmistakable gesture of zipping his gloved hand across his throat and then pointing directly at her.

She felt a terrible icy shock through her whole body. She instantly turned away again, fighting the impulse to run. He wasn't just following her, he was threatening her! But motorcycle or not, he was in traffic and she wasn't. Evasion was still possible. She had just come to a small, one-way street she didn't know, but it was worth turning right onto it, going the opposite way from the one lane of oncoming traffic. He'd have to stop following her now. She didn't look back—she didn't have to. She was walking toward the standing traffic and could easily see that the motorcycle was not daring to fight it and go the wrong way. She was going out of her way now; it would take her longer to get home. But she had managed to evade the motorcycle. For today.

o o o

Supper didn't happen at the same time every day—
her household couldn't be that organized. Because of
the traffic, there was no knowing when Mom or Dad
would get home from work, even though neither of
their jobs was far from their apartment. Mom worked
the day nursing shift at a nearby hospital, and Dad
worked as a home health aide. Her brother, Spencer,
was five years behind her in school, and there was no
knowing when he'd get home either. But by the time
she did get home that day, they were all there already,
which was a little bit unusual. They were all sitting
down at the table before she told them anything
about what had happened with the motorcycle.

Often at dinner Dad and Mom would tell stories
about their patients. Many of the poor people Dad
took care of lived in a pair of substandard high-rise
buildings called the Grand Diamond and the Grand
Emerald. A number of his patients were bedridden,
and Dad had to do a lot of things to take care of them,
including changing them. It made for lip-smacking
dinnertime conversation.

Dad winced a little as he sat down at the dinner

table, clutching at his back. "I don't know what I'm going to do about Mr. Hanumano," he said, shaking his head and sighing. "How much longer can I deal with him?"

"He's the one who weighs four hundred twenty-five pounds, right?" said Spencer.

"Just ask my back," Dad said. "And does he ever even *try* to move a muscle when I have to hoist him over with his swollen dirigible of a tum-tum to get at his loaded diapers? Not on your life! I'll end up crippling myself. And I hate having anything to do with a place owned by that Warren creep."

"Yeah, and who else is going to do it?" Mom said. That was the problem. If Dad refused to take on any patient, it was likely he'd lose his job—and the patient might die. And with the little training he'd had, this was the best-paying job he could get.

They had all heard a lot about Mr. Warren, the rich businessman who owned Grand Diamond. Mr. Warren didn't just own Grand Diamond, he owned lots of other, bigger companies; Grand Diamond was just like a little hobby of his.

Ann knew how much Dad hated rich businessmen

like Mr. Warren. He was always telling the poor people who lived there that the rent was too high, that the apartments weren't maintained enough, that they should refuse to pay their rent until repairs were done. But most of the people were too afraid of being thrown out to do anything to anger the landlord. Ann was tired of hearing about it.

"Something weird happened to me on the way home from school," she said, thinking she would be changing the subject.

They all turned to look at her. "Yeah?" Mom said, a smile flickering around her lips. Mom wanted some comic relief. She had a great sense of humor, and when she and Ann were getting along they laughed a lot together. Once when Mom was driving late at night, and the car could actually move, the two of them were laughing so hard Mom had to pull the car over to the side of the road until their laughter subsided enough for her to start driving again.

"I wish it was something funny, Mom, but it's not," Ann said. "It's creepy. A motorcycle was following me on the way to and from school today."

"Oh, come on. How could you be sure?" Mom could also be skeptical.

"Yeah. So many motorcycles look alike," Spencer said.

"He made a throat-slitting gesture and pointed at me," Ann said, her voice rising.

"What!" Mom put her hands on the table and almost stood up.

"How could you be sure it was the same guy?" Spencer repeated the question to try to stop Mom and Ann from going off the handle.

"I was sure for two reasons," Ann said, angry that they didn't believe her. "The driver was wearing an expensive leather jacket with a pattern of silver studs on it. It was really easy to recognize. But even more than that . . . the bike and the driver's helmet had a weird red logo on it. Not a familiar one that you see everywhere. Somehow I know I've only seen that logo one other place."

"What did it look like?" Dad asked her.

"It was egg-shaped. And the egg was made up of three, like, squirming shapes that sort of looked like . . . like lizards or something."

Dad went pale and put down his knife and fork. "Replico . . ." he said softly, meeting eyes with Mom.

"Replico?" Mom snapped. "Oh, come on, Steve! You don't think . . ."

Then they both turned and looked at Ann.

"What's the matter?" she almost shouted. "What are you talking about? What's Replico?"

"It's Warren's company. Or his group of companies."

"Warren? You mean the same Mr. Warren who owns Grand Diamond?"

"Yeah. But Grand Diamond is nothing compared to the other pots he's got his fingers into. Oil, mainly. That's the big one. Think of all the traffic. He's also into publishing. Big government publishing. Warren's a good buddy with the government. He and the president are both big into oil."

"But why would anybody with his company's logo—" Mom started to say.

"Yeah, that's the weird thing," Dad interrupted her. "He doesn't flash that logo around much. He doesn't want to advertise the fact that all his companies are connected. The only reason I know the logo at all—and the only place I've ever seen it—is on the notices he puts up at Grand Diamond. He's not afraid the poor jerks who live there can do anything to get in his way. So why is he advertising it to threaten *you*?"

Now Mom was getting that hard, angry expression. "Because of your meddling, Steve. And now you're putting your own child in danger because of it."

"You mean because I sometimes try to tell those people to not keep letting him ruin their lives? How could he even know I exist? He's almost never there. He's too much of a big shot."

"That manager you dislike so much is there," Mom said. "The manager's responsible for making sure the building makes a big enough profit. The manager would know of anything that might interfere with that. That's what his job's all about. It's not about making sure the plumbing works or anything trivial like that. It's about making sure nothing interferes with the rent coming in. You've already said the manager treats you like dirt."

"It might have been the manager on the motorcycle!" Spencer said, as if it were a thrilling game. He was practically hopping in his chair with excitement. "And he wants to kill Ann so Dad will stop telling the tenants not to pay their rent!"

"No, not kill her—not yet," Mom said slowly. "This was a warning—the first one." She turned to Dad. "Maybe Mr. Hanumano *is* too much for your back, Steve. Maybe you ought to refuse to take care of him—and let somebody else get involved in that place and the crook who owns it." She sighed, and looked hopeless. "Except . . . what would we do without the money?"

And then Ann remembered where she'd seen the logo before. On a T-shirt. A black T-shirt with the red reptilian egg shape on it.

And the person who wore it was the strange—and yet somehow hot—foreign boy, Lep.

Lep was the boy who had looked at her sympathetically in class today. He wore the T-shirt with the Replico logo a lot—more often than any of the other kids ever wore one particular shirt. She had figured he must be too poor to have very many clothes, and hadn't thought much else about it. She had never thought much about him at all—until now.

His English had been terrible at the beginning of the year—he was obviously new in this country. And this year English was more important than ever, because unless you passed XCAS, you didn't graduate from high school, no matter how well you did in your regular subjects. If you didn't pass XCAS, you had no hope for the future.

Wells frowned every time Lep—Fingernail—wasn't there for attendance. Ann couldn't remember how many times that had happened, since until now there had been no reason to pay any attention to Lep at all. Except that Wells belittled him a lot, because he was afraid Lep would fail XCAS, and that could get Wells in trouble.

English! She hated it so much! It wasn't that she hated reading. Of course she watched TV more than she read books, but she still occasionally did find an interesting book over the summer. And if English class had been like her parents said it was when they were in high school, she might even have liked it, and done well. They read whole books then! And they had conversations in class about the personalities of the characters, their motivations, why the bad guys weren't just evil, but had reasons for the things they did. They had also, apparently, talked about exactly *what* the author did to manipulate the readers' emotions to make them care about some characters and dislike others.

That would have been interesting, even fun, sort of like psychology.

English wasn't like that now. Every minute of English was preparing to pass XCAS. You didn't read whole books by famous authors. You read little selections, a few paragraphs long, rewritten by people at the test publishing company. The paragraphs were too short to be stories about interesting and unusual people having adventures and emotional experiences. Reading was a formulaic exercise. You had to concentrate hard on each word, and all the different things it could possibly mean, because you knew that at the end there would be a list of questions—multiple-choice or essay questions about boring things like the point of view, the main meaning, details, inferences. Your grade depended on how you answered those questions. And some of the questions didn't make sense.

This year they'd had to write an essay on what they did on their snow days, and there had been no snow day at all—and the kids from Haiti and Ethiopia and Thailand had never seen snow. It almost seemed like the whole thing was designed to fool you, on purpose. And the people who wrote the paragraphs were very good at fooling you. Ann was not good at seeing through them. She usually got as many of the questions wrong as she did right.

Ann was a whiz at XCAS preparation in all her other subjects—she often recorded the teachers' lectures with the recorder she always carried in her bag. English was her only real problem at school. And this year it was deadly serious. Because a 50 percent grade wouldn't pass XCAS.

And passing XCAS was the only way out of the traffic.

If you didn't pass senior XCAS you got thrown out of school, which meant you didn't graduate. And if you didn't graduate from high school, you couldn't go to college. And if you didn't go to college, there was no hope of getting away from the traffic.

Mom's alarm clock went off at three A.M. She had to get up that early because she had to be at the hospital by seven on the dot, and with the traffic, it could take hours, and she had to be sure. Their apartment had thin walls, and often her mother's alarm woke Ann up, but she could usually get back to sleep until her own alarm went off at five thirty.

The day after the incident with the motorcycle she couldn't go back to sleep. She lay there for two and a half hours, thinking about the motorcycle, remembering the man's abrupt and violent gesture. She wondered about Replico, and if the threats to her were going to continue, and what her father could do if they did.

It was scary to be singled out by a company as big and powerful as Replico—a company that was clearly above the law if they expected to get away with making threats like that. What if they stopped just threatening her and actually *did* something to her? Even in bed now, she didn't feel safe.

She might be safe if her father quit that job. But then how would they get by? And if she somehow graduated and got into college, how could they possibly afford it? They had trouble making all the payments they already had without college tuition and loan expenses, even though her father *did* have the best-paying job he could get.

All this worry made Ann go from scared to mad. She'd always had trouble controlling her temper. She already felt victimized enough by Wells and XCAS.

She wasn't going to let some punk on a motorcycle control her life and upset her parents.

And what about that boy Lep and his T-shirt with the same logo as the motorcycle? What did he have to do with all of this?

Mr. Wells arranged the seating in his English classes in order of the students' test prep scores. Wells knew the students' exact averages. After all, English class consisted of reading the little selections, answering the questions about them two or three days a week, and being graded right or wrong on each question. So from the first day there was an order of students. Of course their exact test prep scores fluctuated all the time, but Wells didn't waste a lot of time moving the students around. He only went through the long process of changing their positions every Monday. This week Ann was about in the middle—where she usually was—and her friend Randa was directly to her right, in the row lower than hers. Now that Ann was paying more attention to Lep, she noticed with some surprise that he wasn't in the very last place in the English class. In fact, he was in the first seat of the last row, the one to the right of Randa's row. Suddenly he seemed to be doing better in English than she remembered.

He was wearing a frayed white T-shirt, with no logo on it.

"There was a fight on the bus yesterday," Randa told Ann when she sat down just before class was about to start.

"What do you mean, a fight?" Ann said. "What about curity?"

There was always a security guard next to the driver and another one in the back of the bus. "The traffic was so bad they both fell asleep," Randa said, and giggled. Everybody always loved it when security screwed up. "I was right behind these two junior skanks sitting across the aisle from each other, and one of them accused the other one of flirting with her boyfriend. I was lucky to be close enough to hear— they were whispering, of course, so they wouldn't wake up curity. They were hissing every dirty name you could think of at each other—those little girls!— it was the funniest thing that's happened on the bus in ages. And then one of them reached over and just pulled out the other one's pierced earring. A big round one. She shrieked and hit the first one so hard her mouth started bleeding—a bloody mouth and a bloody ear!" Randa was enthralled. "Of course curity was onto them one second later, and had them cuffed, and that was the end of all the fun. Still, it killed a few minutes. And then it was back to reading this drivel." She gestured contemptuously at the photocopied sheets with the English paragraphs on them.

Ann knew all about fights on buses. She had been in a few herself in the days when she had ridden the buses. Her temper frequently got her in trouble. "Of course they'll get detention and points deducted from XCAS scores," Ann said, glancing idly where Randa was gesturing.

Because of where Randa's hand was, Ann noticed it there for the first time, inconspicuous, at the bottom of the test page, very small. The three reptilian shapes squirming together to form the egg.

The logo from the motorcycle that had threatened her.

She felt almost the same icy thrill that had gone through her when the driver made the gesture at her.

Her mind flashed back to the conversation at supper the night before. Dad said he had seen the same logo on notices at Grand Diamond. He also said that Replico—Mr. Warren's group of companies—was into publishing. Government stuff. That's what XCAS was, government stuff. He had said Warren was good buddies with the president, that they were both into oil. And everyone knew the president was one of the main driving forces behind all the XCAS testing.

Publishing XCAS would make Replico a lot of money, since it was the law that every state had to give the tests. That meant buying them from Replico.

The buzzer clanged and jangled. If an electric shock had a sound, it would be the sound of the school buzzers. All the students instantly stopped speaking and came to order. Any hint of misbehavior, any slowness in responding to the buzzers, could mean points deducted from XCAS scores—scores that determined the course of the rest of your life. School was an orderly place these days.

But Ann had made a decision, now that she had seen the Replico logo on the XCAS papers. There were a few minutes between classes—enough time to walk the long hallways to go however far away your next class was, without running, which was of course not allowed. She hadn't been at all sure before, but now she knew she had to talk to Lep during that time. And nothing was going to stop her.

As regimented as school was—students following the buzzers, being seated in order of their test prep scores—the teachers also had tricks up their sleeves. You could never relax because you never knew whether any given day was going to be a practice test day, meaning you had to study the paragraphs every night, just in case you'd be tested on them the next day—or maybe several days later. Today was not a test day, it turned out. So Ann might have wasted her time reading and concentrating on yesterday's deadly dull paragraphs about two men dropping masks from bullet trains going at different speeds in opposite directions, and trying to figure out how far the masks would go and if either man would be able to catch the other man's mask. Of course, everybody knew you couldn't open the windows of bullet trains, but the people who wrote the XCAS paragraphs didn't care about that—accuracy was not their concern.

Trickiness was. Ann had puzzled over the paragraphs for a long time, wanting to ask her father for help but not wanting to disturb him as he dozed over his book. So they weren't going to have to answer questions about those paragraphs today—but that didn't mean the questions might not be flung at them unexpectedly sometime next week, when they had forgotten about the bullet train paragraphs.

Today, instead, Wells was passing back the last sets of questions, the wrong answers clearly marked in bold red slashes. It took time to pass the papers back, because of the way Wells did it. He gave the whole pile to the first student in the first row, the one at the head of the class for that week. That student looked through the papers until she found hers, and then passed them back to the student directly lower. That way the ones who did best got to see all the mistakes of the ones who did the worst. Yes, it took some time, but Wells seemed to feel the humiliation of it was of worthy test-score-improvement value.

And the better Wells's students did on XCAS, the more highly regarded Wells would be by the administration. And if his students didn't do well, he'd be in trouble. It might affect his salary—or even his employment at the school. Being so insecure, he couldn't afford to let any kid disgrace his good name. Ann was sort of surprised that Wells hadn't thrown Lep out of his class at the beginning of the year, when he had been in the last seat, because his low scores would bring down the class average. But recently, oddly, Lep seemed to be doing better.

Ann wasn't sure she liked it that Lep was getting better so unusually fast. She didn't want anybody getting ahead of her. And someone moving up as quickly as he was could possibly push her back.

The paragraphs being passed back now weren't about bullet trains, they were about golf, equally boring to Ann, but—everyone knew—beloved by the president. Golf was just the kind of thing a rich businessman like Warren would probably love too. The funny thing was the really rich kids—the ones who might play golf with their parents—didn't take XCAS, because they went to private schools. Ann, who had never set foot on a golf course, dreaded to see how badly she had done on these. Was there any hope at all of her passing the English XCAS?

She was seated thirteenth out of twenty-five this week. When the papers finally came to her and she found hers, she was surprised to see that she had gotten eight questions right out of ten; she had thought she had done much worse on the golf questions. Would her position in class improve next Monday? Maybe there was hope of her passing the English XCAS after all.

Then Wells droned on about the stupid mistakes the lowest ones in the class had made, and explained how totally obvious the correct answers were, and hinted at the dangerous consequences of being at the back of this class—there was no lower senior English class, and if you got bumped from this one, there was no hope. He also complained about how their teachers last year had not prepared them adequately for XCAS—the test pitted teacher against teacher. There were even stories about teachers cheating for their students so that the students would do better, and the teacher would look better. Some teachers hadn't come back this year. Had they been fired because their students hadn't done well enough on XCAS? Was Wells afraid that would happen to him?

One time when Ann was passing the teachers'

lounge, she overheard Miss Donovan saying to Wells, "I'm glad to be retiring. There's no joy in teaching anymore."

While Wells ranted, Ann and Randa occasionally exchanged scornful glances, but very, very surreptitiously; Wells had sharp eyes, and neither of them needed any points deducted.

Ann wasn't thinking about what Wells was saying. She was going to have to be fast after class to have time to talk to Lep. And she was thinking hard. She knew she would have to come up with an explanation for Randa. And it wasn't going to be easy.

The buzzers singed the air at the end, and Wells stopped abruptly in mid-sentence. The students all stood up and quickly gathered their papers together. Randa started to walk out of the room beside her.

"Listen, Randa, I've got to go talk to that kid Lep," Ann said.

"Huh? What in the world do you have to say to *him*?" Randa wanted to know, as Ann had expected. Lep was not exactly the coolest person to hang with.

She had come to the decision that she couldn't tell Randa about the Replico incident. Of course Randa would tell everybody they both knew, even though she would first swear to secrecy, and then all those people would tell everybody *they* knew. It was just too crazy and violent a story, and had so many weird implications, for anybody to be able to *not* tell it to everyone they could. But Ann didn't want it getting around the whole school. She already felt too exposed.

"You know how my mother gets on these kicks and won't lay off. She thinks I'll do better on the English XCAS if I help somebody even worse than me. And who could be worse than *him*? You know they're going to make him take the same test as everybody else, even though he's foreign and can hardly even speak the language. And Mom got a bonus at work so she's going to *pay* me, so why not? Anyway, he'll probably say no; I'm counting on it." She flashed Randa what she hoped was a reasonable facsimile of a smile and took off after Lep.

Of course there was no danger that Lep would spread her story around the school. He didn't know anybody who mattered, as far as she knew, and nobody knew him.

He was already out in the corridor, walking fast. She brushed past other students in the crowd and caught up with him. "Hey, Lep, wait a second," she said, just behind him.

He turned around, surprised, frowning a little. Almost all boys her age were taller than she was, but he was short, the same height as she. "Yes? Ann?" he said, the dark eyes in his brown face squinting in suspicion. She hadn't expected him to know her name. And she realized, for the first time, that she didn't even know what country he came from.

"Look at this," she said, pointing at the logo at the bottom of the page of English paragraphs.

He didn't understand, the logo was so small. "The English paper? What about that?" he said.

"It's not the paper I want you to see. It's this. This . . ." She didn't think he would understand the word "logo." "This . . . *design* here." She moved her finger around it. "I've seen it before, this design." She took a deep breath. "Don't . . . don't you have a T-shirt, a black T-shirt, with this design on it in red?"

He just stared at her, still puzzled. Was he dumber than she had expected, or what?

"Lep, this is important," she said, aware that they had very little time and trying not to be impatient. "Yesterday, when I was on my way to and from school, a man on a motorcycle followed me. This same design was on his motorcycle and his helmet. The same design that you have on that T-shirt. And then the man *threatened* me!"

His expression still didn't change. It was as though she were speaking to a statue.

"Lep, the man with this design on his motorcycle went like *this* to me!" She repeated the throat-slashing gesture. "And I knew I'd seen this design someplace before, and then I remembered it's on your shirt. And I just wondered if you knew—"

"I don't know! Not my fault! I don't do anything!" he said, angry and defensive. And he took off down the hall, immediately lost in the crowds of students.

She couldn't believe it. This poor skinny boy from some Third World country, who nobody wanted to be friends with, was running away from *her*?

And on her way home from school that day the black motorcycle with the red logo followed her again. She tried not to look back, after the first time she saw him, but she couldn't help it. And as soon as she did, he made the throat-slashing gesture.

3

Elise Warren was getting ready for a date with one of those boring rich boys her father expected her to go out with—though none of them was as rich as she was, of course. She had her own spacious marble bathroom, attached to her large, elaborately decorated bedroom. Before she showered, she made sure her bedroom door *and* her bathroom door were both locked. Then she stuck her finger down her throat. She wanted to be as thin as possible for this date, even though the boy was boring. It was important to her to look perfect at all times.

She knew her parents wouldn't hear anything—they were downstairs in the conservatory having cocktails. It was a school night, but her father still wanted her to go out with this boy because he had important connections. And it was never wise to disobey her father. Not for a trivial thing like this date, anyway. She saved arguing with her father for important things. She was the only person who ever dared to disagree with him.

She showered and washed her hair with imported French lavender shampoo. She wrapped herself in a large fluffy towel and dried her hair with her new hair dryer—she got one every couple of months or so, whenever a fancier, more expensive model came out.

Then she strolled into her walk-in closet and picked out an outfit—tight jeans, prefaded, and a pink silk top that clung to her body. She went through her racks of shoes. Should she wear high heels or not? She tried to remember how tall this guy was—she had never gone out with him before, and he went to a different school. She didn't want to risk being taller than him, so she wore flats—Prada ballets, with a buckle, one of many pairs that she had—that matched the pink color of her top.

It took her about a half hour to do her makeup,

with brushes and creams and unguents, all of them the top brands. She studied herself carefully in her three-paneled full-length mirror for about five minutes, to be sure everything was perfect. It was. She went downstairs.

She entered the conservatory, which was all floor-to-ceiling windows and huge tropical plants. Her parents looked up at her from the TV—they were watching a business report that her father followed religiously and her mother had to sit through because that's what her father wanted.

"Uh . . . do you think that outfit might be a little tight, dear?" her mother said.

"She looks great," her father said roughly. "It's the perfect outfit." Of course he wanted her to look alluring, so that the boy with good connections would like her.

Her mother couldn't argue. She looked back at the TV and took a sip of her drink, a cocktail in a stemmed glass garnished with an orchid.

Now that Elise was about to go out with a boy her father approved of, and he liked the way she was dressed, she said, "Could you please take me with you the next time you go to that building? Grand Diamond. Is that what it's called?"

Her father sighed irritably. "Why do you care about that place?"

She wanted to go to that "place" because a few weeks earlier, waiting in the car for her father to finish some business at Grand Diamond, she had seen the building manager. He was blond and rough-looking in a way that was very attractive to Elise. Then he had winked at her over her father's shoulder, and she had felt a thrill that no prep school boy's smile had ever given her. She was determined to see the man again. But her father's reaction wasn't good tonight. This wasn't the moment to ask him if she could visit Grand Diamond after all.

And then, just in time, she heard the sound of the boy's helicopter landing on the tarmac behind their house. "There he is. Gotta go," she said, and kissed her father lightly on the cheek, which she knew would calm him down. Then she headed for the big front door—she knew the boy would get out of the copter and walk to the front door to ring.

As she waited by the door, she thought about how

far she should let him go in the back of his copter. Not very far, she decided; she didn't like him much, and her father would never know that she wasn't going to put any effort into impressing him. Not for this spoiled boring little rich boy.

She wanted someone much more exciting.

35

That night when Ann told her parents
the man on the black motorcycle had threatened
her again, her mother got angry at her father. And
when her mother got angry it didn't really matter
who the anger was supposedly directed at—it was
just plain miserable for everybody.

"You were at it again, Steve! Encouraging those
people to rebel, to not pay their rents. Your own
daughter's being threatened and you still won't drop
that stupid lost cause!"

He threw up his hands and shook his head. "I
didn't do a thing."

Her mother made a characteristic sound that

was in between a sigh and a groan. "Oh, what's the use? It's too late now anyway. As long as you're around that building she won't be safe. You've got to drop every patient in that place." She sank down onto the old couch, from a junk store or a dump or someplace like that, where all their stuff was from— Ann's father hated buying anything new. "And if the agency won't accept it, you're just going to have to dig up some kind of income somewhere else. God knows how."

"But I thought they needed *men* to take care of poor people. I thought there weren't enough men doing that work," Ann said. "There must be plenty of people in other buildings who need help."

"Sure, there are plenty of people who need my help, in plenty of other buildings," her father said. "They're just farther away from home."

Farther away meant more time in traffic—more time in the car or on a cheap, crowded bus to save the cost of expensive fuel. The bus would put more strain on his back. And he'd have less time to relax at home.

Ann felt her anger rise. "That's so unfair," she said.

She was the only one in the family who ever dared to argue with her mother. "Why should we have to change our lives just because Dad was trying to help those poor people? Why should that meathead be threatening me?"

"Because rich people don't see it that way," Mom said. "They see it that he's trying to take money away from them. People who have the most money are the ones who want to keep it the most. You ought to be old enough to know that by now."

"I do know it!" Ann snapped back, risking her mother's anger, not able to control her own. Then she paused. "I wonder what Lep has to do with any of this—if anything," she said, thinking aloud.

"Lep? Who's Lep?" her father said. "What kind of a name is that, anyway?"

"He's a kid at school. I don't even know where he's from. He must be from a Third World country because he's dark and obviously poor."

"Do you have to pigeonhole people that way?" her father asked her.

"Why shouldn't she?" her mother said, still in a lousy mood. "Everybody else does."

Her parents argued until her mother fell into an angry silence. She picked up a book and began ignoring Ann's father, who dropped down onto the couch, forgetting about Lep, and picked up his own book. Ann was lucky. She had made a mistake. She didn't want her parents to know about Lep. They'd probably want her to stay away from him, because of the Replico T-shirt. But she wanted to find out *why* he wore that T-shirt.

He wasn't at school the next day. Had she scared him away? Or was it just another of his routine absences? There was no test again today. She almost wished they'd had one so that Lep would lose points and run less risk of getting ahead of her. But Wells would probably deduct points from his overall grade point average anyway, for being absent. Where would he be seated in class on Monday? Where would she be?

Friday night a friend of hers, a guy named Jake, had a party. Jake's parties were great because his parents were rich and they lived in a small but real house with a yard. And Jake gave parties only when his parents were out of town. Of course, no one told that to their parents.

It took a while to get there, because the house was in the rich zone, and commuters would be straggling out there all through the afternoon and evening. She got a lift from a friend named Ariel, who had the use of her parents' car. They went directly from school because of how long it would take to get to Jake's. It might be fun in the car with her friends, even though it would take so long in the traffic. But the best part was that she didn't have to worry about the guy on the motorcycle threatening her today.

Randa and Jeff and Becky were also in the car. And of course Randa had to ask her, as soon as they had all gotten in and started crawling through the traffic, "What happened when you talked to that Lep kid yesterday?"

"Nothing," Ann said quickly. "He didn't want to talk to me. Anyway, it's none of your business."

"Well, excuse me!" Randa said.

"Whatever," Ann said, and shrugged.

"Who's Lep?" Jeff wanted to know.

Ann liked Jeff. He was somebody she'd definitely

go out with, if he ever asked her—and there weren't many boys she wanted to go out with. She was picky about who was smart enough and cute enough. She wanted to strangle Randa for mentioning Lep in front of Jeff.

"He's this weird Third World kid in our English class," Randa said. "Ann had some crazy idea she was going to tutor him in English or something."

"I told you it was my mother's idea!" Ann corrected her.

Randa was in the front seat, next to Ariel. Ann was in the back—Jeff was in between her and Becky. Jeff was pressing his leg against hers. Was he doing that to Becky too? Ann wondered.

"But English is your worst subject, Ann," Becky pointed out. "Why would you want to tutor somebody in English?"

"It was my mother's idea!" Ann said again.

Randa laughed. "Believe me, this Lep kid is worse. He hardly ever says anything in class, and when he does, you can hardly understand him."

Ann had already been mad at Randa for bringing up Lep at all, and now she was angrier because of the way she was putting him down—even though she probably would have said the exact same thing about him.

"I didn't know you had problems in English," Jeff said to her, pressing his leg a little more firmly against hers. "Maybe I could help you."

Ann didn't know whether she liked that or not. She would like to spend time with him, but not talking about those stupid English paragraphs! And she didn't like him thinking she was stupid at something. "I did better on the last test," she said. "Let's see where Wells puts me on Monday."

She was hoping something would happen with Jeff at the party. But when they finally got there it turned out Jake's parents weren't out of town after all—they had decided not to go because his mother had a headache. He hadn't had a chance to text everybody and cancel, meaning his parents were not only there, putting a damper on everything by their presence, but they were also mad at him for inviting everybody over when he thought they were going to be away. The party was a boring disaster, everybody left early, and Ariel dropped her off before Jeff, so they never had a chance to be alone together. She had sort of hoped he might call her over the weekend, but he didn't.

On Monday Lep was back in school, wearing the Replico T-shirt. What did that mean? Was it a message to Ann? Or was it just that it was the only clean shirt he had that day?

She noticed now how loose it was on him. He was skinnier than she had realized. His thin face made his eyes look bigger.

The seating in English was reshuffled. Ann was moved from the third row to the second, probably because of doing better on the golf paragraphs. So she wasn't next to nosy Randa anymore, who was still in the fourth row. But most amazing—and chilling— was that Lep had moved up from the first seat in the fifth row to the first seat in the third. Two rows at once was a huge jump; it hardly ever happened. It was especially surprising because he had missed class on Friday. He was ahead of Randa now! This was unheard-of. What had he done to have improved so much so fast?

And what if he got ahead of Ann?

Wells called Lep "Fingernail" when he moved him, frowning suspiciously. He was making it clear to everyone that he suspected him of cheating, for which he could get thrown out of school. Lep kept his eyes lowered.

After their seating was changed, they had a test. Ten questions on the paragraphs they had been assigned over the weekend, which had been about warring middle-eastern space stations. Ann knew she did really badly, but at least she wouldn't be next to Randa for the rest of the week. And after class she just avoided her and waited to approach Lep until he had turned a corner and they were probably lost from Randa's view.

She wasn't as blunt as she'd been on Thursday. She didn't want to scare him away again. "Congratulations about doing better in English," she said to him, once she got his attention.

"Oh. Thank you," he said, not meeting her eye. But at least he wasn't running away from her like before.

"Are you studying more, or what?" she asked him.

"I study more when I have time. When not working."

"You have a job?" She wasn't surprised. She could see that he was poor, and it looked like he didn't get enough to eat. She was more curious about him now. A job could be the reason he was absent so often. "What kind of job? Where do you work?"

He was frowning at her again, as though he didn't understand why she was suddenly interested in him. She didn't blame him; it must seem strange. At the same time, he couldn't have forgotten what she had said about the man threatening her, with the same logo as the shirt he was wearing; he must know that that was at the root of it all.

"I work at place where I live. Where I get this shirt." It was the first time he had mentioned the shirt himself. She was beginning to hope he might be more open today.

"That's the shirt I remembered! Do you mean . . . you live and work at Grand Diamond?"

He seemed surprised, now looking openly at her. His cheekbones stood out because of how thin he was. "How you know about Grand Diamond? Nobody like you live there."

"My father works there. Or he used to, anyway.

I think he might have to quit—I don't know what's going to happen."

"Your father work at Grand Diamond?" he said, more puzzled than ever now.

"He takes care of sick people, in their apartments in that building."

Lep stopped walking abruptly; two kids behind almost bumped into them, looking angry. But they were only sophomores, so all they did was mutter and pass by.

"That man *your* father?" Lep said.

She shrugged. "Yeah. My father. What's the big surprise?"

"But that man . . . But my boss say he . . . That man is your *father*?" He was still not moving; she watched the strange play of emotions across his narrow face. And she saw something that surprised her a little. This kid Lep respected her father. He respected him *a lot*. And that made her feel a whole lot different about him. Almost as though he might not be so dumb after all.

"He helps sick people who don't have insurance and who can't afford to pay somebody to come. But he might have to stop working there, because of what I told you the other day. About the man threatening me. On the motorcycle with that design on it." She gestured at his T-shirt.

He looked down at it. Now she knew he wasn't stupid. He was just evasive. He was scared of something.

"If you live and work at Grand Diamond, then maybe you know if there's a man there, maybe the building manager or somebody like that, who drives a motorcycle with that same design on it. That man has something against me. And . . ." Now she was the one to look away. "That man is mad at me. He acts like he wants to hurt me. And it's going to make things really tough for my father, if he has to stop working there and—"

The warning bell bleated. They were right next to a loudspeaker and the sound was almost deafening.

"We have to go," she said. "But I need to find out more—for a lot of reasons. Maybe we could meet after school. Right outside of Wells's room." She couldn't think of any place else. "Just for a few minutes. Will you be there?"

"I . . . But . . ."

"Only a few minutes. Please?" She did her best to smile; she knew boys liked her smile. "I'll see you there after school." And she hurried off.

For the rest of the day she wondered if he'd be there. He seemed to be opening up a little. And he actually lived and worked at Grand Diamond, and knew who her father was. And respected him. That meant he probably knew—for *sure*—who had threatened her on the motorcycle. And why. And if she had an answer, she might be safer. And her father might not have to drop all his patients at Grand Diamond and get in trouble with the agency, and have to work someplace even farther away in the traffic.

So she was very disappointed when she got to the doorway of Wells's room after school and Lep wasn't there. And he didn't show up, even though she waited, feeling very conspicuous, until the hall was almost empty.

5

Why wouldn't she leave him alone? She
was suddenly being so pushy! If only she hadn't
noticed his shirt!

But she was so beautiful. And she was in so much
danger.

Just when things were starting to get better for
him, just when there might be a little hope, she had
to remember that shirt. If only he had never worn it.
But there were many days when it was the only clean
shirt he had. And how could he have known that man
Mr. Forrest was her father?

The man Tony hated so much. Tony, his boss.
Tony, the only hope he had of improving his life.

Ann was so lovely. He had been admiring her ever since he had been let out of the juvenile detention center and started going to this school. He had never dared to hope he could get to know her, of course, but he had watched her from a distance. And then last week the impossible had happened, and she had come up and talked to him. If only it hadn't been about *that*!

Lep had been put in the juvenile detention center soon after he had come to this country and taken XCAS for the first time. He could barely understand English then, and had answered certain questions in a way that made the security people suspicious, thinking he was a threat to this country. So he had been put in a school that was locked up, with bars on the doors, and all the other students were thieves and fighters. Everyone had to wear the same orange uniform and walk in a straight line, guarded by policemen. Welcome to America!

That he had been singled out by the test to be sent there made him think of an old saying from home: "The nail that sticks out is the one that gets hammered."

He had been stuck in that place until Tony had

found him there and offered him a job, and his family a better place to live. Tony wanted someone from the detention center to work for him. And then Tony started helping him, and Lep understood better how to answer those certain questions on XCAS preparation tests that were put there to catch people who they believed might be dangerous. He had started at this real school last fall. And that's when he had begun to notice Ann.

Lep also walked home from school because it was the fastest way of getting there. Tony wanted him to be at work by no later than five. That meant he had to walk fast, almost jogging, with his heavy backpack of schoolbooks. He had to get up at four to work before school, and at the end of the school day he was always tired when he had to start the long jog home, to more hours of heavy work, and after that, schoolwork, if he could stay awake.

It was very hard. But it was his only hope of getting a better life. Mainly because of Tony, and the XCAS test.

If Tony ever saw him with Ann, there would be trouble.

So of course he couldn't meet Ann after school. It had been a mistake to even let her talk to him. He didn't need her problems interfering with his life. Even though now he knew how serious her problems were—much more serious than she seemed to realize, even as worried as she was.

He couldn't afford a watch, and clocks around the city were rare, so he was never sure what time it was, and whether he would be late, and how angry Tony would be. Tony had been away on his errands Wednesday and Thursday of last week, and Lep thought he would be away on Friday too, so he had taken it a little easier. But Tony hadn't been away on Friday, and he had been in a terrible mood because something had gone wrong with his plans, and as usual he had taken it out on Lep, giving him even more work to do, and dirtier jobs than usual. He was lucky it had been Friday and he didn't have to do his homework after work that night.

So now he didn't dare hope Tony might not be there. He had to hurry home as fast as ever. It was good that it was Monday, when he was fresher and stronger than later in the week, after the long hours had taken their toll.

Sometimes he thought he might just give up and stop trying for a better life. It sure would be easier not going to school! He would be able to rest a little more, but also have time to work more hours and make more money. If he didn't go to school he might even begin to gain some weight, and not stay so thin all the time.

But he would keep going as long as he could. He didn't want to be stuck the way his sister and her husband were, and those kids at the detention center. He had hopes. And to have hopes, you had to pass XCAS.

The test-answers opportunity offered by Tony was just too incredible a piece of luck *not* to take advantage of. He had told his sister about it. She understood about the test, and she knew everything he told her had to be a secret. But no one else could know.

As he hurried past the trapped cars and into the even worse traffic closer to where he lived, he tried to congratulate himself on what was happening in English class. He had done so well on all the tests last week—perfect scores on all of them!—that Mr. Wells had moved him up two whole rows! Was there a chance he might actually be able to pass the English XCAS and graduate from high school? Then life would really open up for him. He tried to bolster his spirits about that and feel proud of himself.

But he didn't really feel proud. First of all, there had been that funny look on the teacher's face today when he had seated Lep at the head of the third row, and called him Fingernail, which Lep knew he meant as an insult. He was going to have to be more careful in the future. Suddenly getting perfect scores all the time was too suspicious—even though he *loved* cheating on that horrible test. He had forced himself to get a few questions wrong before, but last week he had let himself go, because he knew all the answers. He couldn't do that anymore, or he'd get caught. And if you got caught cheating on even practice XCAS, you got kicked out of school, for good.

And the other thing that brought him down was the situation with Ann. Should he try to help her? *No!* he told himself. *You have enough problems already. Don't hurt your own tiny chances by trying to help her. Would she help you?*

Most of the people who lived in Grand Diamond were from other countries, and many of them were from Thailand, like Lep. They could talk about Tony without him knowing what they were saying. There were times when that could be very important.

Nicky, the receptionist, was also Thai. Nicky spoke excellent English—she had to, because she had to be able to talk to everybody in the building and to the people who phoned. She also had to speak to Tony, of course, and even at times to Mr. Warren, on the rare occasions that he came to check things out there—sometimes with his wife.

Mr. Warren had been there on Monday the week before last, in a very bad mood. Lep had gotten there just before Mr. Warren left, in time to hear him say a few last angry words—words Lep had trouble understanding. After Mr. Warren and his wife had gotten in their big BMW, Tony had smiled and lit a cigarette. "We've got a lot of work ahead of us, Lep. Or anyway, *you* do." He pushed buttons on his fancy cell phone while Lep waited. Then Tony gave some orders into the phone that Lep didn't understand at all. He hung up. "They'll deliver the plywood tomorrow. Then we'll get to work. I might have to do some of it too. He wants it done fast. But the faster *you* work, the more I can help you with test answers."

"What he want?" Lep asked, dreading the answer.

"We're blocking off Grand Emerald. The people who live in Grand Emerald will have to use their own entrance and stairs, instead of coming through this one and using our elevator."

Grand Emerald was another building, owned by Mr. Warren's brother, connected to Grand Diamond. The elevator was in Grand Diamond, but people in Grand Emerald could use it by going through the open connecting doorways—until now.

"He don't want them to use elevator? What about people on twenty floor?"

"Good exercise," Tony said, and laughed. "You know the buildings only connect on every fourth floor, so we only have to block off six doorways instead of twenty. No point in mopping the floors or cleaning the elevators today—they'll just get dirty again tomorrow. So today I'll have to relent and let you fix the toilet in five-thirty-two. Those people better appreciate how lucky they are—their toilet's only been busted for a week . . ."

Lep wanted to ask him again why the doors had to be blocked off so nobody in Grand Emerald could use the elevator, but Tony liked to be secretive, and mentioning the test answers was a warning for Lep not to ask anything.

When he had finished fixing the toilet he took a shower in the little bathroom next to the parking garage. And then Lep went into the reception area to find out what was going on. You could usually depend on Nicky to know the gossip.

"Warren's wife told me something about it. She trusts me for some reason," Nicky said, and giggled. She had short hair and was quite pretty. "There was a golf tournament at their country club. Warren's brother did so much better than Warren that Warren was mad as hell. So now nobody in Grand Emerald can use this entrance—or the elevator." The phone rang, but before she picked it up she said, "Warren's getting back at his brother by punishing all the people in that building."

So the next day Lep was nailing up plywood for hours, feeling guilty every time somebody from Grand Emerald saw what he was doing, and walked through the still-open doorway to the elevator Lep was closing off. But he had no choice. And now the people in Grand Emerald had to use the stairs. The old and fat ones were out of luck. That's what life was like if you didn't pass XCAS.

And Tony had rewarded him for doing so much work—and especially for not asking any questions—by giving him some very important papers that he could memorize for school. Papers Tony had been able to get because he worked for Mr. Warren, who owned the company that made XCAS. And that's why Lep was now doing so well on the English XCAS practice, which was the hardest for him. Screw Mr. Wells and the test!

It was the elevators that got that man, Mr. Forrest, who took care of sick people, in big trouble with Tony.

Lep had helped Mr. Forrest once by translating for the sick old lady next door. Nicky had told him more about Mr. Forrest. He went around telling people they should complain about their broken toilets and refrigerators and hot plates to Tony. He said they had rights. And then Nicky put her hand to her chest. "He even tells them *not to pay the rent* if their toilets or electricity don't work." Her eyes were wide with shock, but also because she was impressed. "He doesn't seem to understand what Tony—and Mr. Warren—are like."

After they had blocked off the connecting doorways to Grand Emerald, Lep went and talked to Nicky a minute more. "I can tell you, I'm *very* nice to Tony, no matter what. And Mr. Warren and his wife too," Nicky said. She lowered her voice. "And you'll be nice to Tony, Lep, if you know what's good for you."

"I know what's good for me," he said, imitating Tony's voice, and she laughed.

Lep was nice to Tony all right, and worked very hard. He did everything Tony wanted.

But a few days after they had blocked off Grand Emerald, Nicky was full of more stories about Mr. Forrest. "He's so mad at Tony it's like he's going crazy," she said, shaking her head, her eyes wide. "He's telling everybody in Grand Emerald to tell the police! He says he'll do it if they don't. And not to pay their rents. Of course, most of them are too scared to tell the police, or do anything else. But if Mr. Warren finds out, Mr. Forrest is going to be in big, big trouble."

"Yeah, but what can they do to Mr. Forrest? He's just helping people."

She rolled her eyes. "Grow up, Lep. They don't care about who he helps. All they care about is money. They'll get him somehow, if they decide to."

Lep knew what they were like. Last spring Tony had told him to fix the wiring in 823 so that a fire would start in the room. He knew enough not to ask why. It was Nicky who had told him Tony wanted the woman who lived there to move because she was always late on the rent, and complained about every little thing. She worked as a waitress and had a four-year-old daughter who had to be alone a lot, and after the fire she was too scared to stay there. Tony had given him the special T-shirt for doing such a good job.

And Tony had also given him XCAS answers for the first time.

And what if the little girl had died in the fire Lep had arranged? Tony wouldn't have cared at all. Lep was sure he would want him to do something else like that. And then he told him to loosen the railing on the balcony in an eighth floor apartment where four little kids lived. He was part of it now.

Lep didn't want to hurt anybody. But it made him feel good to get away with cheating on XCAS. And Tony had gotten him out of the detention center.

That was Tony's motorcycle with the same design as Lep's special T-shirt. Following Mr. Forrest's daughter and threatening her was just the kind of thing Tony would love. And if Mr. Forrest didn't stop making problems for Tony, he would do more than just follow her. The police couldn't get him; Mr. Warren had deals with the police. Nicky had told him that many times. So Mr. Forrest telling the police about Tony blocking off the elevators wouldn't help anybody; it would only get Mr. Forrest and his daughter in bigger trouble.

If Lep wanted to help Ann, that's how he could do it—let her know she had to tell her father to get out of the two buildings and stay out.

When he got to Grand Diamond after school on Monday—the day Ann had wanted him to meet her outside Wells's room—he saw from the clock at reception that it was five minutes to five. He was just in time. Tony wouldn't be mad. He went right to Tony's little office, near the bathroom off the parking garage.

Tony wasn't there—just as he hadn't been there last Wednesday and Thursday, when he had been threatening Ann. Was that what he was doing right now?

Lep started mopping the floor in the reception area, which got dirty the fastest. He knew he had to keep busy, whether Tony was there or not, because Tony would know it if he hadn't been working at something.

A few minutes later Tony roared in on his motorcycle. Lep could tell from the way he was revving the engine that he was in a bad mood. Lep hoped it wasn't one of his worst moods. That was when he made Lep clean out people's toilets, sometimes even blocking them himself first so that sewage would get all over the place. It was the job Lep hated the most, wallowing in the stinking muck and sticking his hands into the sewage. He never felt clean for days afterward.

Tony hopped off the motorcycle and wheeled it into his parking place next to his office. He pulled off his helmet. His face was flushed, his white-blond hair wet with sweat. He was in a bad mood all right, Lep could read it all over his face. Lep nodded blankly at him and kept mopping.

"I'm gonna kill that little bitch after what she did today, I swear it!" Tony said, stomping into his office and slamming the door.

Lep and Nicky didn't even dare to look at each other. And of course Lep didn't ask Tony who he was talking about.

He already knew.

Ann waited for Lep for half an hour and then gave up. She felt too weird just standing there. She put on her mask and started walking home.

She had hoped Lep was beginning to open up to her. But now, going over their conversation in her mind, she realized that he had actually told her very little. She had found out that he lived and worked at Grand Diamond, and that he knew who her father was. He hadn't said anything specific about her father, but she still remembered his awed tone of voice when he mentioned him. The way he had referred to her father as "that man" made it very clear that he had great respect for him. Lep knew how much her father helped the people in the building.

He had avoided telling her anything else, such as who his boss was or if the manager or somebody like that had a motorcycle with the Replico logo on it. And then he had stood her up.

Had it been because he didn't have time to meet her after school? Or because he was afraid to tell her anything else?

Her back felt itchy. She looked behind her. No Replico motorcycle—yet.

She got one of the test papers out of her bag and studied it more closely. At the top, in big letters, it said GRATH HULL. That was the name of the publisher. But there, very small at the bottom, was the Replico logo. Meaning Warren owned Grath Hull. She had seen stories on the news about what close connections the president had with this particular publisher. People were always moving from jobs in this administration to jobs at this publisher, or the other way around. And the government decreed that every state had to use tests made by this publisher.

Warren had a really good deal going for him.

And now she saw the test for what it was. Before, she had just accepted it. Now she saw that it was a way of pigeonholing the students, unfairly, to make it easier for the administrators.

She thought about Lep and his frayed clothes and his after-school job. And how skinny he was. Did he get enough to eat?

She thought about the other people in the building her father talked about. That's how people lived who didn't pass XCAS. She felt a familiar emotion— outrage. But this was different. This was outrage against the treatment of people who had nothing to do with her. How could the owner be so unbelievably, cruelly greedy?

And then she thought: *They* do *have something to do with me. They're the reason that man is out to get me.* But now she was just as angry as she was scared. She looked behind her again.

There was the motorcycle with the slimy Replico logo. The guy didn't even wait this time before making the throat-slashing gesture.

Without thinking she gave him the finger.

For a moment he just sat there. She would have

bet that if she could have seen his face behind the heavily tinted helmet his mouth would be hanging open in shock. *Good!* she thought.

She turned and sashayed away from him, swinging her butt just enough to make it clear she didn't see him as a threat. She didn't turn around again.

She felt elated all the way home. And she couldn't wait to talk to her father. She hoped it wasn't too late.

Her father got home later than she did, and he looked more tired than usual. But her mother and Spencer were still not home, which was what really mattered. The first thing she said when her father walked in was, "Dad, did you tell them you had to stop working at Grand Diamond yet?"

He looked puzzled. "Huh?"

"Grand Diamond. Did you tell the agency you couldn't work there anymore?"

He sighed, and lifted his hands guiltily. "I'm sorry, Annie. It's not something you can do in a day or two. I have to figure out a way to get Mr. Hanumano to his doctor's appointment. He can't get out of Grand Emerald without the elevator Warren blocked off."

"Good," she said. "Don't tell the agency anything. Keep working there. I won't tell Mom. I'll tell her the guy stopped following me."

"You want me to leave you in danger from that goon?"

"You want to let those creeps keep getting away with what they're doing to those people? And not just the people in that building, either. Me, and Spencer, and every other kid who goes to school."

He shook his head. "What's got into you?"

"That Replico logo's on all the XCAS papers. You said Warren's publishing company did government stuff. All those tests—all those tests that every state has to buy, that every student has to take. He gets paid for them. He's loaded. And he's still screwing all those poor people who live in that building. We're supposed to let him get away with it?"

He held his palm out at her. "Whoa. Slow down here. Do you know what people like that can do? You name it, any crime they want. They can buy their way out of it. And you think little people like us are supposed to fight them?" He pulled his eyebrows together. "The other day you mentioned some name.

Some 'Third World' kid at school. You wondered if he had anything to do with it. What was that all about?"

"He knows you. He lives and works in Grand Diamond. I think he must know who the guy on the motorcycle is, but he won't talk about that. He's scared too."

"What did you say his name was again?"

"Lep. He's about my height, and dark, and really skinny. I've never seen him wearing anything but old T-shirts—except for the one with the Replico logo on it. He has a heavy accent, but he speaks English well enough so that you can understand what he wants to say."

Her father was thinking hard. "Tell me his name again."

"Lep. But I never even found out what country—"

Her father sat up straight. "Lep! When you said the name before, it sounded a little bit familiar. Now I bet I know who he is. He's a good kid. Thai. He helped me with that old woman, Mrs. Sangsaveng. I couldn't have filled out those disability applications for her if he hadn't translated for me. He works as the custodian in that building. And he goes to *school* too?"

"He's in my English class."

"A foreign kid who speaks like that's in *your* English class?"

Now she knew who she used to sound like—Randa. And why was her father talking that way? "English is my worst subject. We've talked about it. But that's not the point. I know he works at Grand Diamond, and lives there too. And he knows you. But that's all he'll tell me. And the frustrating thing is, I bet he knows what's going on with that guy following me."

Her father stood up suddenly. "Leave him out of it. Don't get him involved. They could kill him and nobody would even know it. And your mother's right. I have to stop working there or they'll do something to you."

"You're just going to let Warren get away with taking advantage of those people?"

His shoulders slumped and he shook his head. "There's nothing we can do about it except get ourselves in deep trouble. You haven't dealt with people like that before. You don't know." He gripped her shoulder. "*Don't get involved!*"

They heard the door open and her mother's footsteps. "You'll get over it," her father said sadly. "It's part of growing up."

But that only made her more determined than ever. She didn't really understand it herself.

She wore her hottest top the next day and she went up to Lep before English class. She didn't care what Randa or anybody else thought anymore. "I gave that guy on the Replico motorcycle the finger yesterday. You know what that means?"

"Finger?" he said, looking uncomfortable.

She showed him, discreetly. He started to laugh, but then held it in. Then Lep met her eyes, very directly, for the first time since she had started talking to him. "Don't," he said, suddenly very serious. "Don't do thing like that to Tony. Make it worse for you, for everybody."

"Tony?" she said eagerly. "That's his name? What does he do at Grand Diamond?"

He looked quickly down again. "You said about

maybe your father leave. Very sad. Help many people. But more safe for you and for him if he go away. Now."

She didn't like what he was saying. But at least he was saying *something*. The buzzer bleated and they had to rush to sit down.

English started out as usual. "You're not studying hard enough," Wells accused the class, his voice rising. "Your teachers last year were too easy on you. Spend more time on these paragraphs!" He shook a bundle of them in the air. "You've *all* got to improve your test scores, even the ones at the head of the class. Do you hear me? And as for those with Limited English Proficiency, what they call 'LEP' . . ." He looked hard at Lep and laughed harshly at the coincidence. "I think it means 'fingernail' in your language, Fingernail!" he practically shouted. "You'll be lucky if you don't get booted out. And if *all* your test scores don't improve I'm failing every one of you!" He was red in the face. He sounded desperate. He stumbled.

And then, so fast that the students hardly knew what was happening, he collapsed to the floor and just lay there, test papers scattered around him.

For a moment all the students sat there, stunned, not moving. It was Ann who finally broke the silence by buzzing the office on the intercom and telling the secretary what had happened. By law, public schools had to have their own Emergency Medical Technicians on duty, since it was so slow for ambulances to get through the traffic. In minutes the EMTs were in the room. They carefully strapped Wells to a board and carried him out, where they would wait for a helicopter to take him to a hospital. The nurse stayed in the room with the students, who were whispering quietly, until the buzzer for the next period went off.

Of course Randa was beside Ann the second it rang. "Can you believe this?" she said.

"Are you surprised?" Ann said. "You know XCAS was driving him nuts. Look, I've got to do something. I'll tell you all about it later." She took off after Lep and tapped him on the shoulder. He spun around.

"I never thought I'd feel sorry for Wells, but I almost do now," she said.

"I never see that happen to anybody," he said, his eyes narrowed. He didn't say anything about feeling sorry for Wells; Wells had been threatening to throw him out of school just before it happened.

"Lep, I've got to tell you something else. If that man on the motorcycle follows me again I'm going to give him the finger again and report him to the cops."

"No!" he said, and for the first time since she'd known him he didn't try to hide his fear. "Don't do anything. Just make your father go away."

"Then meet me after school. If you don't meet me I'll tell the cops about that man. I won't make you late, if you have to get to work. I'll walk part way with you. I can walk fast."

He sighed, and his mouth hardened. "OK, OK!" he said, sounding impatient. "At back door. One most people do not use." And he hurried away from her, losing himself in the crowd.

The back door was a good idea. First of all, the man who followed her wouldn't be looking for her there, so he wouldn't see her with Lep.

And her friends wouldn't see her with him either. Not that it mattered. Randa would be telling everybody that she was talking to Lep instead of her anyway. Ann had always cared so much about her friends. She didn't understand what was wrong with her now. And why had she told her father *not* to quit working at Grand Diamond? He wouldn't listen to her, he'd listen to her mother, as usual. But what if he did listen to her, and didn't stop working there? That guy on the motorcycle wouldn't just keep following her and threatening her. He'd do something worse. They'd already pounded it into her enough that those people could get away with anything. Why was she getting herself into a worse mess than she was in already?

Of course Jeff had to start flirting with her after social studies, her last class. Jeff, who she had really liked for a long time. And she was aware she was wearing her most flattering top. She was frantic, but she couldn't just brush him off like she could Randa, so she had to spend a little time flirting with him, making Lep wait. A week before she would have been thrilled that Jeff was showing interest in her. Now she was just impatient. She couldn't understand it.

After school when she caught sight of Lep at the back door, with not too many other kids around, he was pacing. "Come on," she said. "I'll walk with you. I can tell you're in a hurry."

He walked fast, not meeting her eyes, going in the opposite direction from the way she walked home. "You don't have to worry that guy will see you with me, if he tries to follow me again," she said. "He won't be looking for me on this street. Who is he, anyway? You said his name was Tony?"

"Tony is danger," he said. "Why you don't understand?"

Why did she feel this resistance? Why didn't she want them pushing her around? Why did she care about the people in that building? She had never worried about people like that before.

Could it have something to do with Lep?

She looked over at him. He had dark skin and a flat nose and a black crew cut. His lips were full in his thin face. He held his back very straight, and his yellow T-shirt and blue jeans hung loosely on him. But his arms were wiry; thin as he was, he was strong. She was having a little trouble keeping up with him. What was his hurry? She wondered again why he was so thin. But she felt weird asking him if he got enough to eat. She didn't want him to think she felt sorry for him, that he was an object of pity or anything. She knew he wouldn't like that; he was too proud.

He didn't want to talk about Tony or Mr. Warren—and that was exactly what she wanted to find out from him. He'd only open up if he trusted her. And for that she'd have to use indirect tactics. She knew all about that, from flirting with other boys. "My father said you're from Thailand," she started. "What's it like—"

He turned to her, alarm on his face. "Your father remember me? He know who I am? What you tell him about me?"

"Hardly anything! Jeez!" She shook her head at him. "What are you so upset about?"

"What you tell him? What he remember?"

"He said you helped him with some old lady. He said you were a good kid. He said you worked as the custodian for the building."

Lep was breathing hard now. "You listen!" he said roughly. "Your father don't understand about Tony. He want people in building to tell police!" He stopped walking and lifted his fist. "*No!* If he say anything about me to anybody, ruin everything, my life, my hope. Tell him go away from that building and not say anything about me to anybody, ever, in his life! *You hear me?*"

She was shocked by his anger, even more shocked than she had been by the guy threatening her on the motorcycle, or what had happened to Wells. Shocked, but also more curious than ever. What was going on? Why was he so wrapped up in all of this?

"Lep, listen! My father understands now. He told me yesterday nobody can fight with people like Mr. Warren. He's going to leave that building because he knows it's dangerous. He would never say a word about you. Believe me."

"You make him promise! You hear me? People like you don't understand about people like me. Better if he never go back to Grand Diamond again!" He took off, darting across a packed street before she could think of following him.

She looked around. She hadn't paid much attention to where they were going and wasn't exactly sure where she was. It seemed a little more dangerous around here. She'd better start finding her way home.

Asking Lep about his life hadn't worked. Being direct wouldn't work—he was way too secretive for that. She would have to find another way.

But another way found her first.

She thought hard as she made her way home through streets growing gradually more familiar. The problem was difficult, because she had never known anybody remotely like Lep. He was a mystery to her.

She was also brooding about Wells. It had been a shock to see him keel over like that. Would he die? As much as she hated his class, she *did* feel a little sorry for him.

She wasn't sure when the idea of retaliation became a conscious thought. It must have been just now, after Lep had shouted at her on the crowded street and run away.

What was he afraid of? He worked with Tony every day. What did he think Tony was going to do to him? Why would Tony *want* to do anything to him? Tony was powerful in his world, and Lep was nobody.

She had never felt so stymied in her life. Was she going to have to give in and let Tony threaten her, let him drive her father away from the very people he could help the most? She could hardly stand it. She wasn't ready to accept that life was that unfair.

She was closer to home now, where the traffic was not quite so dense. She wasn't checking as carefully—though she did make sure not to step out into the crosswalk until the pedestrian light came on. She looked both ways and then walked quickly.

It came roaring suddenly out of nowhere, and she felt something—a rearview mirror?—brush against her arm, it was that close. "This isn't the end, you little bitch!" the hoarse voice screamed above the sound of the engine. The motorcycle zoomed around behind a truck, barely missing a collision, and was gone.

But she had seen the Replico logo.

There were no pedestrians around. No cars were

stopping to help. When she reached the other side of the street, her knees were so weak from all the shocks of the day that she knelt on the sidewalk. Her whole body trembled with the rhythm of her heart.

She knew this wasn't going to stop when—*if*—her father left Grand Diamond. It had become a personal thing.

Between her and Tony.

She didn't say anything to her parents about this new attack. She didn't even tell them about Wells yet. She knew she was shaky; she didn't want anybody to notice, so she closed herself off in her room, pretending to study.

But of course she couldn't concentrate. She pondered the whole situation.

Tony wasn't hard to understand. He had targeted her because her father was trying to interfere with his power. And now he hated her, because she had made him think she wasn't scared of him. He didn't like that. So in a way it didn't matter what she did, how deeply she probed. He would be out to get her no matter what. All that did matter was that he *not* know she had any connection with Lep. That would get Lep in trouble.

The main thing she didn't understand was what power Tony had over Lep. Was he afraid Tony would fire him? But why should he worry about that? Tony needed him. He was obviously a good worker, hurrying to get to his job on time, and Tony could probably get him to do that job for very little money.

And yet he had been really terrified, out there on the street, when he thought her father might mention his name to somebody, anybody. So what was he really afraid of? What hold did Tony have over him? What was he using to manipulate him? If she could find that out, she might be able to get him to talk.

And the more he talked, the more she knew, the more power she would have to get back at Tony. And even Warren, in spite of what her father said.

Maybe she could even get them in real trouble.

If she could do it before they killed Lep, or her.

Lep was shaky. He didn't like it that
Mr. Forrest knew his name, or that he and Ann talked
about him. Mr. Forrest and now Ann were Tony's
enemies.

Tony liked having enemies that he could control.
Lep thought of the woman with the four-year-old
little girl, in whose room he had fixed the wiring so
a fire would start. Lep had been the one to do it, of
course. Not Tony. Tony didn't want his hands dirty
with that one, because of the very strong possibility
that the little girl might die. That kind of thing was
Lep's job. But it had been Tony's idea. And Tony
had seemed almost disappointed that nothing *had*

happened to the little girl, and that the woman had just packed up and moved out.

Ann was different. Tony wasn't planning to kill her—not yet, anyway. He was just threatening her, and that was something the police could be paid not to notice. And Tony got a kick out of scaring a pretty girl like that. And now that she was fighting back, making gestures at him, Tony got even more of a nasty kick, because he knew that in the end she would lose and he would win. Her fighting would make him go further. So the more she dared to struggle, the more fun it was for him.

85

Lep didn't want to think about what it would do to his life if Tony had any idea he knew Ann. If Tony had the remotest suspicion that they might be friends, there would be no more test answers. That would be the end of any hope for a better life for Lep. And his sister's family would have to find another place to live. Lep couldn't risk being seen with Ann outside of school anymore, ever again. There was nothing she could do to tempt him.

Except that she was so friendly, smart, and pretty it made his heart sad that he could never know her.

And now he knew that she was not just pretty and spoiled, as he had thought before. She was strong, she was tough, she could fight. He couldn't help respecting her for that, even though she had no idea what dangerous territory she was in. If she died it would be harder for Tony to cover up than if that "Third World" four-year-old girl had died. But Ann was still not important enough that he *couldn't* cover it up, as long as he did it the right way.

And if Lep was the one who did the job, he would have hardly anything to cover up at all.

But how could he ever do that job? It would be the end of everything.

He cursed himself for being so weak to feel that way about Ann. He had to cut that part out of him, to resist all her persistent demands to spend time with him outside the walls of the school. Inside school, Tony could never see him with her.

She had slowed him down a little, but he still got back to Grand Diamond before five. Tony wasn't there, but he was still in a bad mood from what Ann had done to him yesterday. He had left Lep a note that the toilet next to the parking garage was blocked up—

Tony had probably done it himself, on purpose. Lep groaned out loud. That meant wading into the stench and the muck. Lep hated it more than anything. He crept quietly into his sister's apartment. Adoon and Omsin, his nephew and niece, were watching TV, the volume turned down almost to silence. They knew enough not to make any noise when their father was trying to sleep. Lep went to the tiny green plastic dresser in the corner that held his few clothes, next to the little mat he slept on, and changed into his oldest T-shirt and shorts. He collected an extra set of clothes for when the job was finished.

Lep went down to the little bathroom. The floor was covered with sewage. He pushed the plunger into the toilet. It was quicker than he had expected; the golf ball Tony had thrown into it came out easily enough. Then Lep had to clean everything out with a shovel and a mop, doing his best not to breathe through his nose.

His sister, Ing, and her husband, Komron, had come to this country a couple of years before Lep. When Lep was fifteen their parents had died in a motorcycle accident, and Ing had to bring him over.

She said he could go to school for one year, and that was it. And he would have to work too. They lived in an even smaller room than in Grand Diamond. At school, Lep had taken his first XCAS and had done so badly on it that they put him into the juvenile detention center.

Tony had spotted him there as someone poor and illegal he could push around, and had hired him, and offered them the room at Grand Diamond. It was more expensive, but Ing took it because now Lep would be earning money. After Tony had asked him to fix the wiring in that woman's apartment, he knew Lep could report him. That was when he had started bribing him with the test answers. And that was when Lep realized he had a chance of finishing high school, and maybe even going on to more school after that—maybe a technical school or someplace where he could learn a real skill, so he could get a decent job, as an electrician or something like that, and not have to work from eleven P.M. to seven A.M. as a security guard like Komron. Or from seven A.M. to nine P.M. like Ing, cleaning hotel rooms. Ing and Komron hardly ever saw each other and made very little money. Lep wanted something better. He was perversely lucky that Tony could use the test answers to bribe him to do jobs like this and, even more importantly and worse, jobs like setting up the fire that could have killed the little girl.

If only Ann wouldn't wreck all his plans for him! He felt terrible for yelling at her today, for scaring her away. But he didn't know what else to do. In another world, in some magical place, he might get to know Ann some day in a real way. To be her boyfriend, maybe? He cursed himself for even thinking about it. That wasn't real! That was a magical place that could never happen. It would do him no good to even let such an idea enter his head.

Just when he had finished cleaning out the bathroom and was covered with filth, the motorcycle rumbled into the garage. Of course, it was because of what Ann had done to Tony yesterday that he was being punished this way. But he didn't resent her for it. He *liked* her for having the guts to stand up to Tony the way she did, crazy and dangerous as it was, and resulting in this disgusting work for him.

"Enough of that, Lep!" Tony called out to him a

few minutes later. "Get clean so I can talk to you without puking, and come into my office."

Lep threw the filthy clothes in the plastic basin that was used for that purpose only. Then he scrubbed himself under the rusty shower, which had no stall or curtain, and half the time the hot water hardly worked, which was hard in the winter. But today it felt wonderful! And Tony must be in a decent mood for inviting him into his office. What had happened? It could only be good news for Lep. Clean, in fresh clothes, he knocked softly on Tony's door.

"Come in, come in, Lep!" Tony boomed, and Lep knew he was in a good mood just from the ring in his voice. Lep stepped through the door.

"Well, I scared the living bejesus out of that little bitch today," Tony bragged, lolling in the chair behind his desk, puffing on a cigarette, his white-blond hair in handsome disarray. "Her father won't be coming around here anymore stirring up trouble after that. And I'll make sure the next *health aide* that damned busybody agency sends is a helpless wimp who minds his own business."

"What you do to her?" Lep asked, trying to make his voice as blank as possible.

"I sat there waiting where I knew she had to cross the street, and she didn't see me, and then when she was crossing I went so close to her I nicked her pretty little elbow. She was so shaken up she couldn't even stand when she got to the other side." And then he laughed so hard it turned into a coughing fit and his face was bright red as he stabbed out his cigarette.

"Did you . . . hurt her?" Lep couldn't keep from asking, though he knew it was risky; he didn't want to give Tony the idea that he cared what happened to her. He was also furious. How dare Tony do something as dangerous as almost run her over?

But Tony misinterpreted the question. "Not enough so that anybody can pin anything real on me. Barely touched her. But she'll go crying home to Daddy and he'll keep his ass away from here from now on. And now bossman's coming over with the missus. Get busy mopping reception. I got the feeling from his call that he's got some special job—that might earn you some special answers."

Lep knew that "special" jobs were the worst ones—the most illegal and dangerous, like fixing the wiring to start a fire or loosening a balcony railing. They were the ones that got him the largest number of answers for XCAS.

What would Tony do to him and his family if he ever found out that Lep was friends with Ann? Another one of the million reasons he had to stay away from her.

But how *could* he stay away from her if Tony's threats were getting more vicious? Was he going to have to do something to help her?

Elise Warren's pink stuffed bunny alarm
clock tinkled delicately at seven thirty A.M. She
yawned and rolled for a moment or so among the
fluffy stuffed animals on her bed. She knew she was
a little old at seventeen for stuffed animals, but she
didn't care. She liked them. And if the friends of hers
who saw them thought anything was odd about it,
they wouldn't dare to say it, even to each other. They
knew she had ways of finding out.

She got up, slipped out of her mauve silk
nightgown, and took a sip from the glass of freshly
squeezed orange juice, nestled in its tub of ice, that
had been silently placed on her bedside table before

she woke up. She strolled into her bathroom and her large, glass-enclosed shower, with its array of different sprays and different marble seats, in varying shades of rose and lavender. She didn't have to adjust the water temperature; it was always perfectly adjusted for her. When a new maid came, she learned quickly what exactly the right temperature was, because Elise got very angry when it wasn't correct.

It wasn't a hair-washing day so she used the sprayer that cleaned just her body. When she was clean and fresh she found a newly washed, fluffy lavender towel just outside the large shower stall and luxuriantly dried herself. Birds twittered in the flowering trees just outside her large open windows. She brushed her teeth with the electric toothbrush and studied her skin. No new pimples. They had been a serious problem for a while until her father had finally found the right dermatologist, who had the special—and most likely illegal—pills that made her skin flawless. She took her time doing her face. The helicopter— and the headmistress—would wait for her.

She wasn't stupid—she knew she was not really beautiful. But she was smart enough to understand that with beauty, it was the whole package—especially attitude. She also had access to every cosmetic treatment in the world so that her perfect skin and hair and sculpted nose and lovely clothes gave the *appearance* of beauty. And enough rich and handsome guys were interested in her to prove it.

There weren't any guys at her high school. She went to the Andrew Academy, a private all-girls school. There were a lot of reasons for going to a private school—a better class of friends with important parents, more highly educated teachers, almost automatic admission guaranteed to nearly any college. But most important was that at private schools they were not required to do the XCAS tests her father published. The last thing in the world her father would have wanted would be to inflict those awful tests on *her*.

She strolled around inside her closet, pausing to study the various articles of clothing like someone in a shop. She had made it clear from the beginning that she would not go to a school where the students were required to wear uniforms, so that their relative degrees of wealth could not be displayed by their clothing.

Why shouldn't she wear beautiful clothes? Why shouldn't the other girls envy her? She picked a pink cashmere sweater that she knew would look good on her with her padded bra, and a pair of perfectly faded jeans that were just exactly the right size for her to be able to squeeze into. There weren't boys as students at her school, but there were frequent activities with boys from other private schools. And her bathroom at home was large and private enough so that she could easily throw up without being detected whenever she ate anything the least bit fattening. She was proud of her eighteen-inch waist, and she knew it emphasized the figure that she so carefully created with her special dieting methods and the exercise machines in her gym next to her bedroom.

Her father was at the table in the dining room, which had French windows looking out into the garden, lush with spring flowers. They never ate in the kitchen. It was for the staff, after all, and she could hardly remember the last time she had been in it. Her mother was not up yet, of course; she rarely left her room until noon. At her age, it took her a lot longer to get ready to make any kind of appearance.

Elise's father was sipping his coffee, having finished his bacon and eggs. She didn't like him eating fattening food like that, but that was one of the areas over which she had no control with him. He was short, only five foot six, and it was easier for short people to develop a paunch, and he had one. She wasn't happy about that, but she knew where to draw the line with him. Lucky for her that her mother was tall, five foot ten, and she took after her.

Her father looked up from the financial papers, dapper in his white shirt, blue suit, and blue-and-silver diagonally striped tie. "Morning, baby," he said, and smiled slightly at her.

"Morning, Daddy," she said. She knew that calling him Daddy, like having her collection of stuffed animals, was a little babyish, but he liked it, and with her father it made sense to make a few concessions and do some of the things he liked. Then he would be more likely to give into other things. Anyway, he never expected her to call him that in front of anybody else, so what did it matter?

She sat down to her bowl of nonfat yogurt and fresh wild blueberries and oranges. Gloria had heard her come down, of course, and in a moment brought her the steaming little pot of specially imported green tea.

"I'm afraid you're going to have to have dinner by yourself tonight," her father said. "Your mother and I have to go see to that damned building again. I'd sell that nuisance if it weren't for Buddy. But he'll never sell *his* building, and I don't trust him to handle it right. It was a mistake to ever give it to that idiot. Sometimes I'm too kind for my own good." He sighed.

"I'm still so curious about Grand Diamond," Elise said. "Couldn't I go with you and help you with your business? I want to learn more about what you do." She hoped this sounded convincing. She felt her cheeks flush but not at the lie so much as the thought of the blond manager.

Her father frowned. "How would you get there from school?" he said. He didn't sound particularly encouraging of her sudden interest in his work. She had an answer.

"Why can't the helicopter just take me to Grand Diamond? Why don't *you* ever take a copter there?"

"The roof isn't strong enough. Haven't I told you that? No point in throwing good money away on a building like that, when we don't go there very much."

"Couldn't the copter take me somewhere where you could meet me in the car?" she said, frowning prettily. She pushed her bowl away, having eaten only a couple of spoonfuls. "If I can't go, I don't know if I feel like eating." Threatening not to eat often worked with him.

He sighed. "But you don't understand, baby. You'll just die of boredom. I have to talk business with Tony, the manager, and your mother has to go over things with Nicky. And, and . . ." he spluttered, and shook his paper irritably.

Tony. She liked the name. She knew what was bothering her father. He didn't want her to hear what he talked about with Tony, seeing as how it was most likely illegal—that was why her father had to go to the trouble of talking to Tony in person and not over the phone which could easily be tapped. And by personally making periodic checks on the building, he gave the impression that it was up to code.

She often wondered if he had any idea how much she suspected about his illegal activities.

And why did her mother even bother sitting in traffic to go to the building at all? Who was Nicky?

"I don't feel good," she said. "I don't feel like eating and I don't feel like going to school." The skipping school threat was her heavy artillery. Her dad paid a lot for the school.

"What is it about that building?" her father asked her, letting a trace of irritation show in his voice. That let her know she was getting into dangerous territory— though she also knew he would never in a million years treat her the way he treated almost everybody else he had any dealings with. "I mean, it's . . . it's not anything special, really. It was just a little business deal that I'm starting to think isn't worth nearly the trouble it causes. If it weren't for Buddy—"

"If it weren't for Buddy, you'd sell it. You told me that," she said. "And some day you probably will. And then I'll never get to really see it."

"But why do you want to see a place where a bunch of poor foreign losers live?"

"Because you never let me go anywhere interesting!" she shot back. "Do you want me to grow up not knowing *anything* about the real world? What kind of person would I be then?"

"You'd be cultivated and superior and . . . and . . ."

"And ignorant. Do you want to raise a daughter who doesn't know what life is all about?"

"Your mother doesn't—" he started to say, and then caught himself in time. "OK, OK," he said, standing up and tossing his napkin onto the table. "Get out of school early and have the copter take you to my tower. No later than three."

She pulled back the bowl of yogurt so that he would see she was eating it. She always liked winning against her father, because she knew so few people ever did. Maybe the reason he had to win all the time had something to do with being short. She had seen a show on TV once about somebody like that, some old French general whose name she couldn't remember. He had been very aggressive because of being short. Some sort of complex, they called it.

It would also be nice to leave school early. And

maybe—maybe—she would get a chance to talk to Tony.

They had three copters, one for each of them. Her father's tower had a big tarmac on the roof, and he and some of the other wealthy parents had built a tarmac at her school—they didn't want to waste time in the traffic, and they didn't want their kids to, either. (They hadn't *given* it to the school; the school was paying them back slowly, with interest.) Of course, the people who had the copters were car manufacturers, or oilmen like her father, who made money from the people who lived in the traffic, and who also helped to create it. But that wasn't their problem.

Elise loved riding in the copter, and loved being one of the eleven kids at her school who had one. It was wonderful sitting in the cool, plush leather seat and looking out the window at the skyline, and especially down at the cars sitting there, motionless so much of the time, and being aware of speeding over them. Her classmates who didn't have copters had to get up at ungodly hours in order to get to school on time. Those who lived close to her house could have ridden with her, of course—the copter was a four-seater, but her father didn't like to do that. He said it was a waste of gas—every extra pound used up more fuel. Elise liked it that everyone in the school—including the teachers, none of whom had copters of course—could hear whenever hers landed next to the playing fields. She loved getting out of it and strolling toward the front doors, especially when she got closer and could walk past the cars lined up to drop off students, who had been sitting in traffic for hours. Some of the kids probably resented her, but she knew they didn't dare show it: Her father was too important.

She greeted her friends and then went to the head office and told the secretary that she had to leave school at two-thirty, for business reasons. The secretary made no comment except to make a note of it. Miss Smythe, the headmistress, would not be happy about it, but she was in no position to object. If she did, her father's loans to the school would dry up, and seeing as this was Elise's last year there, Miss Smythe did not want that money to dry up any sooner than it had to.

Elise knew she would miss the afternoon social

with the boys at Boggs Academy, which bordered on her school's property. There were several tall, handsome, rich ones there whom she liked to flirt with, and whose parents encouraged this interest in her. She had gone out with a couple of them too. And she knew that Roger Dodds, the last one she had gone out with, would have been glad to get serious with her, but she never let it happen, she just strung him along. She was looking for something much more exciting.

She tolerated math and social studies and American history. English was her most intolerable subject. They were now studying a very long boring book called *A Tale of Two Cities*. They had to discuss the characters and their motivations. Even worse, they talked about what the author did to make the readers like or dislike certain people, and how there were some people who had good and bad sides to them, like this crazy old lady, Madame Defarge. The only parts Elise liked were the executions, but it didn't seem fair to her that it was usually only the rich people who got their heads cut off. Why did so many people think rich people were evil? They were just smart enough to get more out of life.

It was so wonderful at two-thirty when she heard the copter landing outside, and strolled out of class and across to the landing field. She knew other students were watching her out of the windows so she stood as straight and tall as possible and sucked in her stomach—not that it needed much sucking in.

Of course she was treated deferentially at school, but at her father's tower she was a princess. The guards saluted her; the secretaries and receptionists, if they were important enough to talk to her, always told her how great she looked and how beautiful her clothes were. Her father was still busy in his large corner office. Her mother's copter had arrived shortly before, and she was sitting in the private area for important people, flipping through a magazine.

She never really wondered why her mother had married her father; he had been born into money and had already been rich and important when they met in college. So what if he was four inches shorter and getting fat? Still, it would have been better if her father had been tall and good-looking, like some of the other magnates on the TV news. A part of Elise hoped she would end up with somebody who was rich *and* good-looking. But of course she knew that the rich part was more important, in the end. Rich now, however, she wanted good-looking.

Although she knew she was not truly beautiful, she was better looking than her mother. Her mother was tall and thin, but her horsey face was pretty hopeless. She had tried, of course, but there really wasn't much the plastic surgeons could do to fix the essentially long and bony structure of her head. Her nose, her wrinkles—of course they could be dealt with. But the underlying bones of her cranium were too much for them. That's why it took her so long to "put her face on," as she called it. Today she was wearing a red dress that looked great on her, Elise had to admit, and her auburn hair fell in pretty waves to her shoulders.

They had to wait for her father, of course; he was always in important secret meetings. When they finally did leave, they had their own special way out of the parking garage so they didn't have to wait in the queue of people lined up to pay at the tollbooth. But once they got out, there was nothing they could do about the traffic.

Still, they had it better than most people; her father had made sure of that. The car was huge, the chauffeur way in the front, and the rest of it essentially a lounge. The limo was so wide it barely fit in one lane, and was almost as long as a bus. In the back there was a full bar and a TV—they could snack and drink and watch TV and ignore the polluted hell going on all around them. Of course, the drag was that there was only one TV, so Elise had to watch the stupid soap opera her mother was addicted to instead of teen reality shows. Her father whispered on the phone most of the time. Elise was glad she was wearing the cashmere sweater in the freezing, scented air-conditioning.

And yes, the building was seedy inside, as she had expected. The lobby was cramped compared to her father's tower, but then everything was. A short, dark skinny boy in frayed clothes was mopping the floor.

And as soon as they had parked, Tony stepped out of a door close to where a big black motorcycle was parked. He was taller than Elise remembered, taller than her mother, towering over her father. He wore a silver-studded black leather jacket but it was unzipped enough to see the muscles outlined by his tight black

T-shirt; the guy was powerfully built. Elise liked that. And she liked his white-blond hair. It was just long enough, and tousled in just the right way, for Elise to know that he had a spent a good amount of time in front of the mirror in preparation for their arrival. He and her father shook hands, and her father's hand was dwarfed by his big powerful grip. Seeing Tony again sent tingles up Elise's spine.

He made a suggestion of a salute to her mother, nodding and smiling at her, and then he turned to Elise. "My daughter, Elise," her father said. "This is my manager, Tony."

Tony grinned at her. "*Very* pleased to meet you, Elise," he said. "What an unexpected pleasure. What brings you here today?"

The words just came out of her. "I wanted to see my father's special building . . . And to meet *you*."

Her father rolled his eyes a bit comically. "You know how it is," he said. "When a girl wants something . . ."

Tony was still beaming at her, clearly liking what he saw. He was so hot. How could she spend time with him without her parents nearby? Would Tony dare? It would be a big risk for him. On the other hand, he probably knew a lot of things about her father that her father wouldn't want to get around; Tony might have some power in their relationship. She started running ideas through her head. It probably wouldn't be too hard for her to get her hands on his cell phone number. She could usually figure out a way of getting what she wanted, just as she had finally gotten her father to bring her here.

Tony turned away from her, to the little dark boy who was squeezing the mop with his hands. Couldn't her father even provide him with a ringer? Not that she cared about making the job easier for him. It just didn't *look* good for him to be mopping in that way. Behind him, the woman at the reception desk was eyeing her curiously.

"OK, Lep, the floor looks clean enough now," Tony said to the boy. "Finish up next to the desk and then you can go round up all the garbage and load up the Dumpster before the collectors come."

"Elise, go talk to your mother and Nicky. Tony and I have business," her father said.

Of course he and Tony would have business. He

wasn't going to let her spend time with him. She would have loved to hear what their "business" was. But she would find a way.

"That scruffy little dark boy is still around here?" her mother complained to Nicky.

Nicky kept her face expressionless. "Lep is a very good worker, and smart too," she said.

Her mother sniffed.

A harried-looking man with dark hair that should have been trimmed weeks ago came in through the street door. He went straight up to Nicky. "Excuse me," he said to the three of them, smiling politely. "But we kind of have an emergency situation. And since I see that Mr. Warren must be here . . ."

"What's the matter, Mr. Forrest?" Nicky said. She was pleasant to the man, but she also looked worried, almost as though she knew there was going to be trouble.

"It's Mr. Hanumano, in Grand Emerald," the man said. "I thought I might be able to help him get down the stairs, but he just can't do it. And he has an important doctor's appointment, and they're very hard to get when you don't have any money. And I was wondering if . . ." He hesitated. "Well, if it might be possible for Lep to take down just one of those plywood panels, just for a few hours, so that Mr. Hanumano could get to the elevator in this building."

Elise's mother stiffened. "What? After the things Buddy's wife said to me?"

Nicky seemed to care about what the harried, disheveled man wanted. She turned to Elise's mother. "Do you think you could put in a word to Mr. Warren?" she asked her. "Mr. Hanumano weighs over four hundred—"

Mrs. Warren cut her off with a sigh of irritation. "You know I have no influence over Mr. Warren's business decisions," she said, shrugging.

Elise wanted to laugh. Business decision? It was nothing but a childish family quarrel. Elise didn't care about the poor fat man and his doctor's appointment. But it would be wonderfully satisfying to make her parents look so very much in the wrong, which they obviously were. And she could show Tony that she was tough. She suspected he would like that.

"I'll talk to him," Elise said. "Is there a way of calling Tony's office?"

"They don't like to be interrupted when they're having their meetings," her mother warned her, looking scared.

"But this is an emergency!" the disheveled man burst out. "The guy could have an attack. Are you going to let that happen over one piece of plywood?"

Elise loved it that this man, who obviously had no money, was talking to her mother that way. "Give me the phone, please, and tell me the number," Elise said to Nicky. "I bet they won't mind if *I* interrupt."

"Elise," her mother said in a frightened voice.

"Dial one two two," Nicky said bravely, handing Elise the phone.

"But Elise," her mother said, really scared now. "You know your father. He could . . . what if . . ."

Elise dialed. After a couple of rings, Tony said, "Yes? Grand Diamond Management."

His voice made her feel warm. "Oh, er, Tony, this is Elise Warren. I'm *so* sorry to bother you, but—"

"No bother. Not from *you*," he said. "What can I do for you?"

She was thrilled he didn't just hand the phone to her father. She wanted to say, "You could take me for a spin on your motorcycle." But this wasn't the time. She explained about the fat man who had to get to the doctor.

"That's very kind of you," he said, though there was an edge to his voice that she couldn't interpret. "And as a matter of fact, we were just talking about that. Your father decided to have the plywood taken out anyway—lucky for that jerk Forrest. I'll have Lep do that door first. He can take care of the garbage later. Be right there."

"Thank you so much," she said, and hung up. Her mother and Nicky were both staring at her.

"They were going to have that boy take them down anyway," she said, turning to include the disheveled man. "He can just—"

Tony came barreling out of his office. "Don't take this as a precedent, Forrest!" he said to the disheveled man, and Elise was a little shocked, his voice was so different, so outraged. It would be scary if he ever talked to her like that. But of course he never would. "This has nothing to do with you or your patient," he snarled. "We already decided to take the plywood down. What floor is that fat old man of yours on?"

"Eight," the man said without expression.

"Well, you can just go up to all the landings where the garbage cans are and see where Lep is and tell him I said to start taking it down."

The buildings were twenty stories high. She knew her father would never shell out for a cell phone for that boy with the funny name, even one just to use at work. But wouldn't some sort of two-way radio make sense so this man wouldn't have to check out all the landings?

But the disheveled man didn't object. He just hurried out to the stairs.

Tony turned and beamed at Elise, suddenly an entirely different person. "That was very kind of you," he said. And he went back to his office.

"Thank you," Nicky said to Elise. "You know, maybe you saved his life. They wouldn't take that plywood down right now if you didn't ask."

Her mother didn't say anything. She wasn't going to spell out how dangerous it was to interrupt any of her father's meetings, in front of Nicky. But she didn't like what Elise had done. Elise knew she would hear plenty about it later. But it was worth it to make her parents look selfish.

Before they left, the disheveled man wheeled the fat guy out in his chair, a tiny little old woman beside him. He was so disgustingly gross he could barely squeeze into the chair. The rest of the visit was, in fact, as boring as her father had predicted it would be. Nicky and her mother just went over petty accounts. And then there would be the long ride back to her father's tower, the closest place where they could get the copter.

But when they left, and her father and mother were getting into the car first, Tony winked at her again. Maybe something could happen between them after all! Meeting Tony—and getting his phone number—had been worth the whole trip.

The next time Ann walked into English a smiling dark-skinned woman wearing a sun-washed pink shirt greeted her at the door. Ann felt an unexpected brightness. There was no Mr. Wells. He must be really sick at the hospital. It was clear immediately that this substitute was going to be very different. She had a vivid presence, in contrast to the grayness of Wells.

The classroom was configured differently. Wells's desk had been shoved into a corner, and the students' desks were arranged in a circle, with the teacher's chair at one end. Ann hurried to sit next to Lep.

As soon as the bell had screamed, the woman

looked around at them all, still smiling. Wells never smiled—he was always too worried about test scores. "Hello," she said. "I'm Ms. Summers. Mr. Wells will be out for a while and I'll be teaching your English class." She held up some test papers before walking over and dumping them on Wells's desk. "I don't understand all these dumb little paragraphs you seem to be studying," she said as she sat down again in the circle. "I'm an actress, artist, reader, writer, and thinker."

The students looked around at each other, wanting to roll their eyes.

"Why does Mr. Wells concentrate on these little paragraphs instead of *books*?" the woman went on.

For a moment everyone was too surprised to respond. Then Ann—who was feeling outspoken these days because of her campaign to get Tony and Warren in trouble—raised her hand. "Yes?" said Ms. Summers. "And please tell me your name when you answer so I can begin to get to know all of you."

"My name is Ann," she said. "And those paragraphs are what we read to prepare for XCAS."

"XCAS?" Ms. Summers said. "That sounds a little familiar but I don't really understand."

"The test," Ann said, hardly believing this woman didn't know about it. Where had the school dug her up? "If you don't pass XCAS you can't graduate, even if you get A's in all your courses. And the school cares because they rate the schools on the test scores, and if the school doesn't keep getting better test scores, if they don't make AYP, then they—"

"Excuse me, but what's AYP?" Ms. Summers asked her.

Ann felt like saying "Abolish Your Principal," but instead she told her the real meaning: "Adequate Yearly Progress. If the whole school doesn't get better test scores every year, then the school doesn't get as much money from the government. And the teachers get in trouble if they don't get their students to improve their test scores." She paused, and then dared to add, "So that's why Mr. Wells wants us all to do well on XCAS."

"Well, *I'm* not going to get in trouble," Ms. Summers said, sounding a little angry, but not at Ann. "And I don't care if they don't like it. Studying these paragraphs would not be pleasure for anybody. I think you need a break from this . . . stuff." Ann felt she had wanted to say another word to describe the paragraphs. "I'm going to read you a story—one of my favorite stories—and then we can talk about it. It's a long story so I probably won't finish it. I've made copies and you can finish reading it at home tonight for your homework, and then we can discuss it tomorrow. It won't matter if you skip this test . . . stuff for a few days. In fact, I believe it will be better for you in the long run."

There was a slight murmur of amazement among the students. But it didn't last long. They were trained too well.

Ms. Summers sat down and opened a book. "'The Machine Stops,' by E. M. Forster," she said, adding, "You'll be amazed that this story was written in 1909." And she began to read.

The story was about the future. The surface of the earth was too polluted for anything to live there, so everyone lived in little cubicles underground, connected together like a beehive. Everyone lived alone, one person per cell. Their only contact with other people was through a screen powered by something called the Machine. It *was* amazing that this story was written in 1909, because the Machine was so much like a computer, and the people were so much like kids today IM-ing each other. The Machine also supplied air and food and water, and took care of them when they were sick.

The students listened raptly. This was so different from English with Wells! Like Ann, most of them had probably never been read to in their lives. It was amazing how pleasurable it was. You sat there and the story unfolded in your head, as Ms. Summers read it in her graceful voice.

Ann glanced over at Lep. He was listening as intently as everybody else, and because of how clearly Ms. Summers read—she *had* said she was an actress—he seemed to understand everything.

Ms. Summers did not get to the end of the story, but just before the bell she passed out the copies she had made and told them again to finish reading it tonight so that they could discuss it tomorrow.

Ann wanted to make some kind of comment to Lep about how strange this was, but he seemed to be avoiding her. Anyway, she didn't want to lose all her other friends. So in the hall she walked with Randa.

"I wonder how they could let somebody like her slip by them?" Randa said, shaking her head.

"Well, I'm glad they did," Ann said. "She's a whole lot better than Wells and those stupid paragraphs."

"But . . . being read to?" Randa muttered. "Doesn't that seem sort of babyish? And what about our test scores?"

Ann stepped in front of her and stopped. "Did you dislike it?" she said. "Do you dislike that story?"

Randa's eyes fluttered away from her. "Well, actually . . . it's kind of enjoyable. Like watching TV in your head."

They started walking again, both thoughtful. "In a way, it's almost better than TV," Ann said. "No commercials. But mainly because everything is happening inside your mind. So there are no limits. You can picture anything."

That night Ann's father seemed more tired than ever when he came home. The agency had moved him to a different building that was farther away than

Grand Diamond. But he had gone back one last time to check on Mr. Hanumano. Tony had seen him there and yelled at him.

Mom's face went hard. "You went back to Grand Diamond? After everything that happened? And Ann being threatened by that thug?"

There was silence around the table for a moment. Then Spencer said, unable to hide his excitement, "Do you think he'll start threatening Ann again now?"

"You should have told him you were never going back there," Mom said. "Why didn't you do that? To protect your own daughter!"

Dad shrugged. "I just left. I couldn't stand listening to him yell at me. I'll never go back there again. Tony will know that. Ann will be perfectly okay."

But he didn't sound sure of himself. Ann wasn't so sure either. Then something happened that made the danger very clear and very great.

They ate at a cheap barbecue place near their apartment that night. And on the way home they saw Tony, with a girl riding on the back of his motorcycle. Her father was shocked. The girl was Warren's daughter, he said. And Tony knew they had seen him with her.

Ann was worried, but she still finished reading "The Machine Stops" that night instead of watching the usual TV sitcoms. The main character in the story was a woman named Vashti who began to worship the Machine like a god, as most people did. But she had a son, Kuno, who was a rebel, and who insisted that she actually leave her cubicle and fly in an airship to visit him in person—he wanted to talk to her *not* through the Machine. And when she saw him he told her he had gone to the surface of the earth, climbed up by himself through ancient dark ventilation shafts used by the workers who had built the Machine, when men could still breathe the outer air. He had to break the cover of the shaft in order to get out onto the surface. He had not died up there. But the Machine's mending apparatus, huge things like worms, noticed the hole in the shaft and came crawling up and dragged him back down into the dark again.

His mother was infuriated by what he had told her and flew away immediately and cut off all contact with him. Later she heard that he had been moved away from that area so he could not get out again, to a cell very close to hers.

Then, as the title said, the Machine—upon which everyone in the world depended for everything—began to fail. It was like the hard disk of life gradually crashing. There were gasping sighs in the music. The food tasted bad now, the air started to smell rotten, the lighting got dimmer and dimmer. Lecturers on the screen kept praying to the Machine, but of course that didn't do any good. Beds failed to appear when summoned. Communication broke down, and nobody could talk to anybody else. Dying people crawled out of their cells into the corridor. Finally everything fell apart and airships came crashing through the cubicles and everyone was going to die.

But at the very end, amazingly, crawling in the darkness, the woman heard her son's voice. And he told her what had really happened when he went up to the surface. There had been people there, people who had adapted to the conditions, people who lived without the Machine. Which meant that even without the Machine, there was still hope that the human race would survive. For some weird reason it made Ann feel like crying. TV never did that.

o o o

Ann was nervous about Tony when she started the long walk to school in the early morning. She kept looking behind her. And when she got closer to the school, and it was full daylight, there he was. And this time he stopped ahead of her, so quickly she couldn't think of what to do, and pulled up the faceplate of his helmet, which he had never done before. He was young and good-looking, with white-blond hair.

And he was holding a knife.

He didn't seem the least bit worried that nearby people in cars or on motorcycles would see him with the knife. He held it up at her, running one finger lightly along the gleaming blade as she started to run.

She was panting when she reached the school. And she didn't know what to do. Should she tell Lep about this, or not? She brooded about it constantly through all her classes before lunch, and in the end decided it would be better not to tell him. Telling Lep about the new attack would only make him even *less* likely to confide in her. At lunch she and her friends laughed and gossiped as usual. Nervous as she was about Tony, Ann was still able to put on a good act.

And then she felt a brief touch on her shoulder. She turned.

"Excuse me," Lep said. He looked extremely tired, the skin around his eyes even darker than the rest of his face. But he stood up straight and met her eyes. "Can I talk to you, please?"

He had never been this assertive before. She liked it. She didn't care what her friends thought. She picked up her tray and went with him to an empty table.

"Do you know, your father come to Grand Emerald yesterday?" he asked her.

"Yes," she said.

"I think he come to see how is Mr. Hanumano," Lep said. "But Tony see him. Tony hate more than ever now."

"But my father's never going back there again."

Lep's voice went soft. His eyes widened. "But Tony still hate. I see it, I feel it. I know Tony very well." He looked down, not meeting her eyes. "And I worry about you very much."

She could hardly believe it. It was almost as though he were letting her see that he cared about her. And in a way she never would have believed, that actually made her feel she might care about him.

Him? Lep? To care about him in the way she should be caring about Jeff? She never would have believed it. But would Jeff worry about her in a situation that could be so dangerous for him—a situation like the one Lep was in?

He glanced at her, then looked away. "I know Tony since first I come to this country," he said. "I see how he can hate people, very, very deep. If your father never come back he have no more reason to hate you, but I don't know if that mean the hate going away." And then he looked back sadly at her face and touched her hand, very briefly and lightly, just a flicker of a touch—not like the way Jeff grabbed onto her hand when he was flirting with her the other day. "I think you still . . . need to be very careful."

Lep moved his hand away. Ann felt like holding on to it. What was the *matter* with her? What was going on here? "What would happen to you if Tony found out you know me?" she asked him, without thinking. It just came out of her.

His face closed up instantly. "Not think about

that. Not ever. Can never go out of this building with you again."

Still, he didn't get up and walk away from her, as she was sure he would have done before. But she knew that he would if she pursued this line of questioning. She decided not to tell him that her whole family had seen Tony the other night, or who they had seen him with. That would probably scare him away for good. And she didn't want to scare him away, ever again. She was going to have to be very careful and gradual with him, not like with her other friends.

Her "other" friends? Did that mean Lep was her friend now? Or was it something else? It felt like something else. She looked at his serious face and she felt something she had never felt before. She felt what it might be like to be him, with everything in his life a struggle. Not that her own life was that easy. But for him, it was clear that everything was harder. It wasn't something he would want to talk about, she could sense that. Again, it was his pride. And it made her angry to think that people could treat him like he was second-rate.

"Why does Tony think he can do that to me? Why

does he think he's above the law?" she asked him. "It's not fair."

"Fair?" For the first time since she had known Lep, he laughed. He shook his head. He beamed at her and his smile lit up his face. "I think . . . I think you are OK," he said softly. "I don't think you are stupid. But don't you know? Money is everything. If you can pay, can do anything. Just make it secret."

And here he was saying this, who had only old clothes, who didn't seem to get enough to eat, who had to work after school. And she hadn't even finished her salad. Of course she couldn't offer him the leftover food—he would never accept it. She didn't know what to say.

He didn't say anything for a moment, then looked quickly up at her. "Don't walk to school alone anymore. Find boy walk with you, boy who live near you. I can't help you."

He already knew Tony would be out to get her. So why shouldn't she risk telling him what had happened this morning? There was a chance it would jolt him into telling her more. "Tony already did it," she said. "This morning, on my way to school. And he had a knife." And then she just blurted it out. "And last night my whole family saw him with Warren's daughter on his motorcycle."

Lep just looked at her miserably. She reached out and touched his hand. "But he won't ever see my father again. Mr. Hanumano is doing better now. My father will never go back there again. Not after this. I'll try to find somebody to walk with me."

Lep stood up. He was upset that they had seen Tony with Warren's daughter. "I go now," he said. "Find boy walk with you."

"Wait," she said. "Did you read that story for English?"

He looked relieved. "Yes!" he said proudly. "I read whole story. Take me long time because I read English very slow, and long, hard words in that story. But I stay up all night to read it, because I like the story very much, and I like the new lady teacher. So much better than before!" He stood up even straighter than usual. "And I am tell her too."

The bell screamed, and he was gone.

For the first time in her life, Ann was looking forward to English class.

11

Elise knew she was playing with fire.
And she loved it.

Tony was so hot! And the fact that her father
would be beside himself with rage if he ever found
out only made Tony hotter.

It had been surprisingly easy. Nicky had given her
the number of Tony's office at Grand Diamond. And
of course it was easy to get the main number of the
building. There were only four phone lines for the
two hundred rooms in the building. All calls had to
go through Nicky, and of course most of the time the
lines were busy because there were so few of them
for so many people. You just had to keep dialing

the numbers one after the other until one of them happened to be free. But once she put the numbers into her cell phone, all she had to do was press one key to dial each number. It had only taken her half an hour on Sunday to get through. And once she did, she knew Nicky wouldn't recognize her voice.

"Grand Diamond," Tony said in his husky voice that made her shiver.

"Hi, Tony," she said. "This is Elise."

"Elise?" he said.

"Elise Warren. We met the other day at my father's building."

"Oh! Oh, er . . . hello," he said, sounding nonplussed for such a cool guy.

"I'd kind of like to see you again," she said. "I mean, just the two of us. Nobody else has to know about it. Ever. There must be places we can go where no one will ever see us." And then she held her breath.

"Well, it, uh, might take a little arranging," Tony said, hesitant.

Of course she had known he would be reluctant. If her father ever found out, he'd lose his job. He didn't want her going out with men like Tony. It wasn't just that Tony was too old—though he was as much of a hunk as any movie star. Her father wanted her to be dating guys from their own wealthy social class, guys who would grow up to be building owners, not managers. And she was perfectly happy to waste enough time going out with boys like that to satisfy her father.

But what she really craved was excitement, and Tony was all excitement. She could tell from looking at him in his tight T-shirt that his muscles didn't come from a gym. He worked with his body, with his hands. He rode a big powerful motorcycle. He was the boss of the building, not the soft owner in some perfect office tower lounging around talking on the phone. He got that little foreign kid to do all the really ugly dirty work for him. But she knew from what her father said that he was good at building things, that he climbed up on ladders to fix things. He was strong and tough.

And her father was his boss, so she would be in control. She liked to be in control. She was in control of her parents, even though they didn't know it, and she was in control of her teachers, who did know it. And now she wanted to be in control of a tough guy like Tony.

"You can pick me up after school on Monday. My parents will be out of town. We can meet a few blocks from my school so nobody there will see us." She made her own voice husky. "I *really* want to ride on that motorcycle of yours."

"You're sure your folks will be out of town?" he asked her.

If it had been anybody but Tony she might have been a little miffed that he distrusted her. "They left already. My father has business in D.C. next week." It was the truth. "Check it out," she added. "Think of some reason to call him tomorrow. His secretary will tell you."

"I don't know where your school is. Where do you want me to meet you? I don't want nobody from the school seeing me."

She loved his ungrammatical speech! She gave him directions to a corner where nobody would spot them and said she'd be there at four P.M.

When the copter pilot, Henry, dropped her off

on Monday morning she told him not to pick her up, she was going to a friend's house and they'd give her a ride home. He raised his eyebrows. If he said anything to her father, it would be easy for her to lie about it—her father didn't know the names of all her friends at school.

She was so excited that it was hard to act normal. She would love to brag to her friends about the kind of guy she had a date with that evening, but she forced herself not to. If anybody else knew about her and Tony there was the remotest possibility it might get back to her father. And if it did, Tony would never want to see her again. She knew how much power he had in that building. It would be hard for him to find another job like it. And if he got fired, he would blame her. Danger was part of Tony's excitement, but she didn't want that danger focused against her.

She got to the corner—not near any of the boutiques or the hangouts—at quarter to four. It was at a city bus stop, where nobody from her school would be caught dead. She was generally very sure of herself, but now she felt a little nervous. What would happen if he didn't show up? Not only would she be hurt and insulted, but she'd have a lot of trouble getting home on her own. She kept checking her Rolex, trying to look casual and inconspicuous. People stuck in traffic glanced over at her, but they would just think she was waiting for the bus.

Four o'clock came and went and there was no Tony. She kept glancing out onto the street to see if his motorcycle with the red logo was there, and then quickly turning away. She didn't want him to catch her looking for him.

She heard a roar, and turned back to the street, and there he was on his bike, one booted foot on the curb. He pushed up the faceplate of his black helmet and grinned at her. She knew she looked good. She was wearing another tight sweater and one of her padded bras and jeans that hugged her like a second skin.

"Hey, babe," he said, and again he made her tingle all over. He patted the seat behind him. "Hop on," he said.

The government with its tight security enforced most things, but one thing they didn't enforce was the law that passengers on motorcycles had to wear helmets. She liked not wearing a helmet. It made the whole adventure even riskier. She climbed onto the bike, trying to look as though she did it all the time, though actually she had never been on a motorcycle before. Once she got on she eased herself forward, wondering how close she should get to the back of Tony's black leather jacket. He reached around and grabbed each of her hands in one of his and pulled them around his abdomen, tight. The muscles on his stomach were solid and hard, not like any of the boys she had gone out with, even the athletes. "Now you hold on tight, babe," he said. "Don't want you falling off when we really get going. Where to?"

She would have liked to get out of the city, but even on a motorcycle that would take so long that she'd get home so late the staff would surely tell her parents when they got back. Tony probably had to be back at the building in a few hours too. But if they just stayed on choked streets like this they'd never be able to get up much speed. On the ritzier streets that she was familiar with a screaming speeding motorcycle might cause some attention. But Tony probably knew the city better than she did. "Somewhere where we can go fast," she said. "And then we can get something to eat."

"Gotcha," he said, pulling down the faceplate of his helmet, and maneuvering the bike out into the traffic.

It was great holding on to his lean, muscular body and weaving around and getting ahead of all the cars. The pollution was unpleasant, though. She wasn't wearing a mask because she rarely needed one, going to and from school in the copter. And she hadn't wanted Tony to see her with a mask covering up her perfect skin. She hoped he knew some place to go where they could get out of the traffic and go fast, the sooner the better.

It was fun when they got to the first red light and worked their way up to the very front of the line waiting for it to change. Now they were surrounded by other motorcycles, which were always in the front. She was happy to see that Tony's was one of the biggest and fanciest; she was riding higher than most of the other girls. And when the light changed they zoomed forward and she caught her breath at the wonderful speed of it, until they reached the next line of cars and had to start weaving around them again.

Because they could work their way ahead of the cars, it was not long before they came to a park she had never been to before, seedy and run-down. While they were waiting at the traffic light before the entrance she could see oddly dressed people sitting on benches in the park, some with shopping carts filled with stuff in old plastic bags. She had never seen anybody like that before. They must be the homeless people they had been taught about in school. She wondered vaguely what they did when it got cold. But only vaguely. They were not her problem.

When the light changed she forgot about them completely. There was no traffic in the park! Apparently the streets in there didn't lead anywhere, and the people in the cars were all on their way home or to some other place that the park wouldn't take them to. Tony gunned the engine and they were off.

She had never experienced anything like it. Wind whipped past her face and blew her hair back wildly. The roads in the park curved and when Tony went around a corner the entire bike tilted way to the side.

It was thrilling, even scary, like a fabulous amusement park ride. But it was a lot more fun than a stupid ride because this really *was* dangerous—people died in motorcycle accidents all the time. She clung to Tony's rigid stomach even harder, wanting to scream out something for the sheer joy of it, but not wanting to act like a child. It was more exciting than she had expected.

She would have been glad for this to go on for hours, but in what seemed like a very short period of time (she had always noticed that fun went fast and boredom dragged on forever) Tony pulled the bike over to the side of the road and lifted up his faceplate—it was impossible to talk above the roar of the engine when they were going fast.

"Like that?" he asked her, removing his helmet to brush back his beautiful hair.

"It was the most fun I've ever had in my life. I want more! I want to do it again," she gushed, panting slightly in her excitement.

He chuckled. "We'll do it again, babe." He looked at his watch. "But I gotta get back to the building soon—no getting something to eat this time."

She was disappointed, but at least he had said "this time," meaning there might be other times.

"The problem is getting you home," he went on, his brow slightly furrowed. "I can't take you, you know that, somebody might see me. I'll take you as close as I can, and then I'll have to get a taxi for you."

"Sure," she said, smiling, wanting to appear agreeable, even though she had wanted to spend more time with him, get to know him better, get him to want her. But now he was implying that that would happen, and her parents did go out of town a lot.

"I know a place where it's always easy to get a cab," he said. And then, quickly, he shifted around in the seat and put his hand on her neck and kissed her. The rough feel of his lips was wonderful, nothing like the babies she went out with.

It was after the park, while they were at an intersection, that she saw the harried-looking man from Grand Diamond. Tony looked over and saw them too. The man was with his family, a tired-looking woman and a pretty girl her own age and a young boy. And the man saw Elise, for sure; he looked right at her with a surprised expression. He got a good look; they were weaving slowly.

Who was he? He had been helping one of the poor dodos who lived at Grand Emerald, trying to get him to the hospital. Was he there often? Did he ever talk to her father? Would he tell him he saw her with Tony on his motorcycle?

The light changed and they moved away from them.

She was going to have to get rid of that man, fast, and she was going to have to do it through her father. But how? And how could she find out about him without creating suspicions?

Now she was worried. That stupid man had taken her euphoria away.

She thought again. No, her father was too risky. She would get him through her mother. Her mother was pretty dim and might not suspect anything. And she would know who the man was because she had been there. Once Elise knew who he was she would know how much danger Tony might be in from her father. She didn't want Tony to worry about that man because she wanted to do this again and again. She wanted fun and excitement, and Tony was fun and excitement. And if in the distant future it resulted in him losing his job, the staff would protect her from him. She wanted to ride with him and be with him and do anything with him as many times as possible before it inevitably ended.

Neither of them said anything about that man seeing them. Elise acted normal when he dropped her off. He was right, there were a lot of cabs here, and she got one right away.

And all the way home she thought about that man and his family, and how she could stop him from causing her any problems.

12

"Here's the first and most obvious question," Ms. Summers said as English class began. "Can anybody tell me what the Machine reminds you of?"

Lep shot his hand up. It was the first time he had raised his hand in any class since he had come to this school at the beginning of the year. He wondered why nobody else raised their hands. This was an easy question. Ms. Summers nodded at Lep and said, "Before you answer, please tell me your name."

"My name Lep," he said, feeling shy, but looked her straight in the face. "And Machine like computer. Like people who sit all the time at computer, and never see other people, and don't have real life. Good story."

"Exactly," Ms. Summers said, smiling. And even though Lep knew the question was easy, he couldn't help feeling pleased.

"If you lived in that world, how do you think you would feel about it?" Ms. Summers asked the class.

Lep looked around. Again, none of the other students raised their hands. And then Lep slowly raised his.

"Yes, Lep," Ms. Summers said. "You seem to be the most responsive student in this class."

He didn't know what "responsive" meant, but he knew the answer to this question.

"I want to think I hate that world, like man Kuno," Lep said. "But maybe not. Because somebody who grow up there, from baby, think that only way to live."

"Very astute, Lep," Ms. Summers said.

Lep couldn't help glancing over at Ann. She was smiling at him. She looked like she might even be proud of him!

"I wish some other students would be as wise

about this story as Lep is." Ms. Summers paused. "Let me tell you something interesting about this story. It was written *before* World War I. Most writers of speculative fiction at that time believed that technology would only help mankind; that it would create a utopia where they would be free of manual labor and could spend their time on higher things. It was only after the horrors of World War I that they realized how dangerous technology could be. What do you think could have alerted this writer, E. M. Forster, to the dangers of technology in *advance* of the war?"

That was hard. Lep had no idea of the answer. How could she expect them to know what things were like in 1909?

Ann tentatively raised her hand.

Ms. Summers consulted a sheet of paper and then said, "Yes, Ann."

"That's kind of hard to answer because we don't know what technology they had in 1909. I know they didn't have computers, for sure, and TV, and probably didn't have cars. Did they even have radio then? I don't know *how* that writer could guess about all that stuff."

"How could you find out what they had then?" Ms. Summers asked the class.

A boy near the front of the class raised his hand. "My name is Keith," he said. "And you could look it up on the computer. Like maybe you could search for Marconi, the inventor of the radio, to see if they had radios in 1909. And look up about cars and planes and things."

"Exactly," Ms. Summers said. "You all have computers, don't you?"

Everybody but Lep raised their hand. Ms. Summers noticed. "I saw that they have computers in the school library, if anyone wants to use them," she said to the whole class. "You could do research after school."

Lep was glad she was kind enough not to single him out. But he didn't feel proud anymore. He was embarrassed that he was the only one who didn't have a computer. And how could he stay after school when he had to get back to work for Tony?

But before he did that he would have to check on Ann, to make sure she was not walking home alone. Tony had a knife this morning. What would he have this afternoon?

Their assignment for tonight was to find out what technology they had in 1909. And tomorrow they could discuss it and try to figure out what had given this writer the idea that technology could be dangerous. It was an impossible assignment for Lep. And he had been so proud of reading the whole story! Now what was he going to do?

He could tell Ann wanted to talk to him after class, but instead he went up to Ms. Summers. He wanted her to understand. When most of the kids were gone he said to her, "I'm sorry. I have work after school. Sorry I cannot do what you ask. But I did read whole story."

She smiled at him. "Don't worry, Lep. I'm already giving you an A on this story. I can see how smart you are. And you can be part of the discussion tomorrow when the other kids find out a little bit about what technology was like then."

She was kind. But he still felt very shy about being so different from everybody else.

After school he watched for Ann. He wanted to be sure she did not walk alone. She was hanging out with some of her friends in front of the school. He kept hidden behind the statue of a man on a horse. And when Ann left to walk home, she walked alone.

Why hadn't she listened to him? Why hadn't she found a boy to walk with her? He was sure a lot of boys would have, she was so pretty. But she was walking alone.

He couldn't let her do that. He could be late for one day—he would lie to Tony and say the teacher kept him after school. He began to follow her, keeping carefully hidden. He didn't want her to know, and most of all he didn't want Tony to see him having anything to do with her. He didn't know what he would do if Tony *did* try something. But he couldn't let her walk alone. He couldn't let anything happen to her.

The hard part was that she kept looking back, probably to see if Tony was following her. So Lep had to be very careful to keep behind anything—parked cars, lampposts, bus stops—and at the same time not lose her. He had never done this before and didn't know where she lived. He didn't have a watch but he knew he was going to be late, and Tony was already in a bad mood because of what her family had seen, and would be in an even worse mood when Lep showed up late. The day had been so good for a while because of how he had read the whole story and answered questions in class. And now it was getting so bad.

And then there was a motorcycle weaving over to the curb behind Ann. It was not Tony's motorcycle with the red design on it, and the driver was not wearing Tony's usual helmet, which also had the red design. The license plate was different from Tony's too, G571. But he was wearing Tony's jacket. And he had a gun. It was Tony. And this time he was not advertising who he was.

Lep started to shout and run toward them. But Tony was so fast that he shot before Lep even got close. Ann fell. And then Tony was out of there, zooming dangerously ahead of cars into the traffic, brakes screaming.

Lep ran over to her, his heart thudding in his chest. Had Tony killed her? If he had, he would get him. He didn't care what would happen.

And as he approached Ann she sat up, brushing back her hair. He couldn't see any blood. He knelt beside her.

Her face was whiter than ever, her mouth half open. "Ann, Ann, you OK?" Lep asked her, supporting her back with one arm.

She could hardly talk, she was breathing so hard. "He . . . he missed," she managed to say. "I ducked. I didn't feel . . . anything. But I . . . I . . ." She put her head in her hands and started to cry.

He squeezed her shoulder gently, trying not to cry himself. What was he going to do? How could he let Tony get away with this? He would have to tell somebody, and lose his job, his home, his chance of a future.

But how could he prove Tony had done this? There was no direct evidence that the man who shot her had been Tony—no red design, a different license plate. Other people could have a jacket like that. But of course it had been Tony. Why would anybody else want to shoot her? She had seen him with Mr. Warren's daughter.

Lep rocked her gently while she cried, as a few other people gathered around them. Finally Ann looked up, tears on her cheeks, her face very close to his.

"We . . . we have to tell police," Lep said.

"But then . . . If you do that, you'll lose your job. They'll throw your family out," she said, still crying a little. "You stay out of it. I can tell them myself."

He couldn't believe it. Even now, when she had almost been killed, she was still worried about him. It was amazing.

Could it mean she cared for him?

That was impossible. He shook his head to put the idea out of it. But he didn't take his arm from around her shoulders. She leaned against him.

"Hey, you OK?" a man standing above them on the dirty sidewalk said. He had a big fancy camera around his neck.

"I'm . . . OK, I think," Ann managed to tell him.

"That guy *shot* at you. I didn't get a picture. Damn! I didn't get his license number either, he was too fast."

"I remember number," Lep told him. G571 was stuck in his head forever.

"Here." The man gave him a little white card. "I have an important meeting or I'd interview you right now. Come and see me, ASAP. I can help." He hurried away.

"Thank you," Lep said, surprised that somebody on the street would be so kind. Most people ignored everything they saw; they didn't want to get themselves in trouble. Lep slipped the card into the back pocket of his jeans.

Ann started to get up. Lep held tightly on to her upper arm to help her. Her legs were shaky. When she was standing he still held on so she wouldn't fall again.

"But Lep," she said, beginning to get herself under control. "What were you doing here? You always have to rush back to work. This isn't the way you go."

"I follow you. I afraid what Tony do."

"You mean, you were willing to risk your job and your home to protect me?" she said, and started crying again, and threw her arms around him.

He hugged her back, his emotions welling over. "I don't care about job or apartment or XCAS answers Tony give me," he said, without thinking. "I don't want him hurt you."

She held on to him a moment longer. She hiccupped. Then she pulled slightly away, her hands still on his shoulders, her eyes wide. "*XCAS answers!*"

she said, and hiccupped again and wiped her face. "So *that's* what he bribes you with! Of course!"

"Oh," he said, wondering if he had made a terrible mistake. But what difference did it make if she knew? Tony had tried to kill her.

Her face lit up. She was actually smiling now, so soon after what had happened to her. "Lep, that's how we can get them. The president of the publishing company letting Tony give out test answers! We can get Tony and Mr. Warren in big trouble now!"

What did she mean? Get Mr. Warren in trouble? How was that possible? "I don't understand," he said, scared of what she was saying.

"You *know* Mr. Warren is the publisher of XCAS. If it went public that he's giving Tony answers to give to you, to make you work so hard, and maybe do other things too, Mr. Warren would be out of business. It's against the law!"

"Mr. Warren above the law," Lep said, as he had said before.

"About some things, yeah. But not when it comes to XCAS," she said. "People will find out he's a criminal." Her eyes opened even wider. "And it will make the test look bad too! Maybe XCAS might not be so important after this. If people find out about what Mr. Warren is doing."

XCAS not so important? If that was possible, then he would have a much better chance of graduating from high school and improving his life. Now he wasn't scared. "I help you," he said. "I can tell you other thing Tony make me do for XCAS answers. Anything I can do, I help you."

She hugged him again. And this time they hugged each other harder than before. More deeply than before.

13

"Remember when we were at Grand
Diamond?" Elise asked her mother when she got home
from school on Wednesday. She had timed it right.
She knew her mother's second favorite soap opera
would not be coming on for another half hour.

Her mother sipped her afternoon tea—no sugar,
no milk—and took a tiny bite of her no-carb biscuit.
"Do I *have* to remember Grand Diamond?" she asked
Elise.

Elise sighed. "I'm just a little bit curious. Remember that man who needed a haircut and who was
wearing old clothes? He wanted to get that fat man
to the doctor."

"Mmmm," her mother said, barely listening.

"And that other man, the manager, I forget his name, yelled at him." (Naturally she didn't want her mother to know she even remembered Tony's name.) "The manager didn't like him. Do you know who that weird man who cared about the fat man is?"

Her mother yawned. "Why do you care?" she asked her.

That was just what she didn't want her mother to ask. But she was prepared, of course. She knew how to control her parents. "I was just curious because I wondered what he was doing wrong, and why the manager got so mad at him."

"I knew it was a mistake for your father to let you go there," her mother said.

Elise sighed again. "What difference does it make?" she said. "I'm just curious, that's all."

"Your father doesn't like that man either. That's why he's out of the picture now."

Elise's heart lifted. "Out of the picture? What do you mean?"

"They got rid of him. He won't be coming back there anymore."

That was a relief. But she still wasn't sure she was completely safe. "What was his job there, anyway?"

Her mother looked at her suspiciously. "Why do you care about someone like *that*?" she asked her.

Because I don't want to be an ignoramus like you, she felt like saying, though that wasn't the major reason. "Because when I grow up I want to be a businesswoman and run a corporation, like Dad. So I need to understand things."

"He was some sort of health worker. Some little socialistic branch of the government sends in people like that to take care of those people's health needs for *free*. Seems unfair to me that those people should be coddled that way, without paying a penny. Like all immigrants, they expect our government to take care of them."

"Is that why Dad didn't like that man?"

"No, no. He has to put up with having health aides. He can't break that law—I mean, the law." Her mother put her hand to her mouth and made a fake little cough. "But that man went too far. He was telling some of the tenants not to pay their rent!" Her mother's eyes in their mascara opened wide. "*That's* what should be against the law, but for some reason it isn't. And a few of the tenants even complained to Tony. That's the manager's name." She peered more closely at Elise. "But you knew that. You called him up by name and asked him to take the plywood down. And he *winked* at you when we were leaving."

Elise blushed. Her mother had noticed that? Did she suspect anything else? If she did, Tony would lose his job. And then Elise would never see him again. And it was all the fault of that wretched health aide man!

"Why isn't it illegal for that man to interfere with Dad's business?" Elise said, trying to get the subject away from Tony. "Can't somebody do something about it? Do you know what his name is?"

"Why does it matter to you?" her mother wanted to know.

Because I want to make sure he never opens his mouth about seeing me with Tony, she thought. She shrugged. "Because I care about Dad and I don't like people who try to interfere with his business."

Her mother fell for it. "Nicky said his name several times, and Tony said it too," she said thoughtfully. "Woods?"

And then it flashed into Elise's mind—she was quicker than her mother, thank God. "Forest!" she said. "That's what they called him." She hopped up and looked at her watch. "Almost time for *As the Earth Rotates*," she said, hoping the soap would drive this conversation out of her mother's mind. "And I should probably go and do some homework."

She went online. There was no one in the area listed under the name "Forest." But she knew he had to live somewhere not very far from those buildings—he would have no time to get to work in the traffic if he didn't. Was there another way to spell it? The only way she could think of was to put an extra "r" into the name. She looked up "Forrest."

There was only one, a Steven Forrest. She keyed the name and number into her cell phone. She still wasn't sure this was the right one. How could she find out for sure?

At dinner she said to her father, "So you got rid of that interfering health aide guy, Forrest?" She wasn't afraid to ask him this because it had nothing to do with Tony; it wouldn't give anything away.

They were eating roast rack of lamb, medium rare, scalloped potatoes with onions and cheese, and steamed and buttered brussels sprouts. Elise would also be expected to eat dessert. She always planned to throw up after this kind of meal.

Her father took a sip of red wine and put a piece of pink lamb into his mouth. After swallowing, he said, "You know, it really wasn't the wisest thing for you to interrupt my conversation with Tony."

Back to Tony again! Elise didn't like that. "But you got rid of Forrest, right?"

Her father narrowed his eyes. "Why do you care about it?" he asked her.

She wanted to sigh with irritation, but you didn't do that in front of her father. "I just don't like it when people interfere with your business," she said, trying to appear modest and genuine.

"That's the last time I'm ever bringing you there, for sure," her father said.

Fine, she thought, *I can see Tony on my own.*

"But since you ask, yes, we did get rid of him. We have a new one now who minds his own business.

We have to put up with a health aide, but not one who tries to turn the tenants against Tony." He leaned forward. "Your mother said Tony winked at you. What's that all about?"

She was going to have to shut Forrest up somehow. Even though he didn't work there anymore, he was still a threat. And what was she going to say now? She came up with it in an instant. "He winked at me?" she said curiously. "The building manager? Funny, I didn't notice. Why would he do that?"

Her father turned to her mother. "Are you sure about that, *darling*?" he said to her nastily. He was on the verge of being angry, and that was dangerous.

Her mother didn't dare argue with her father. "Well, I thought I might have," she said in a small voice. "But I could be wrong."

"Well, *I* didn't see any wink," Elise lied, furious at her mother for mentioning it to her father. This whole conversation was making her more eager than ever to make sure this Forrest guy would stay quiet.

She called Forrest's number at eight thirty, when he was likely to be home and when it was still not time for even early rising workers to go to bed. A girl answered—most likely the pretty girl she had seen with him. "Can I speak to Mr. Forrest, please?" Elise said politely.

"Who's calling, please?" the girl said, equally politely.

That made Elise mad. And she was already mad to start with. "Just somebody who wants to tell him to mind his own business," she said sweetly.

"Oh, you must be associated with those goons at Grand Diamond," the girl said.

"How dare *you* say something like that?" Elise demanded.

The girl just laughed. And hung up on her.

Now Elise was even more furious. There was trouble coming from that family, it was very clear to her. Not just the father; the daughter too seemed to have something against her father and Tony. And the daughter had seen Tony and Elise together too. She would have to do something about it, without her father knowing. It would be easy to find their address on a map online, and what public school served that area—of course she went to a public school, her father couldn't make enough money for anything better. Shutting them up would be very satisfying.

Her bedroom door was already closed. She went into her bathroom and locked the door and stuck her finger down her throat.

14

Ann was glad she said "goons" to the person on the phone. The person who was most likely Warren's daughter, from the sound of her voice. She was already in real danger as it was, and she had just made it worse. But she was still glad she had said that.

She hadn't told her parents about the call—she didn't want them to worry. Just as she had not told them about Tony shooting at her. If they knew, they would do something, take steps that might interfere with her plans for Tony and Warren.

But she brooded about the call as she lay in bed trying to sleep. And as the situation began to clarify itself in her head, she began to relax a little more.

Warren's daughter must be scared. Her father wouldn't like to know that she had been riding on the violent building manager's motorcycle. Ann's father had said he was glad to be away from that explosive situation. But the girl must be afraid Ann's father might tell her father about it.

Ann smiled to herself. And what would happen if somebody *did* tell Warren about it? It sure would get Tony in deep trouble with his boss. It could be the first step in her campaign. And after deciding that, excited as she was, she was able to sleep.

She had gotten Jeff to agree to walk with her to school. She would have preferred Lep, but he lived in the opposite direction; it would be way too far for him to walk, and he had so much work to do. Anyway, that was impossible because Lep didn't want Tony to see them together. Jeff would walk with her for the next two days, Thursday and Friday. He was pressuring her to come over to his house while his parents were away over the weekend. Now, after what had happened with Lep, she wasn't even considering it. But she could string Jeff along until then. She knew it was mean of her.

But was she supposed to put her life at risk to be nice to Jeff?

Anyway, now she didn't like his carefully styled hair and expensive clothes. All he thought about was himself. Lep really cared about her.

She was able to put on an act and chat happily with him as they walked and the day dawned. But she worried about Tony, and about the weekend. If she canceled on Jeff, he'd stop walking with her. There was nobody else who lived near her. Maybe she *did* have to go over to his house, just to save her own life.

But now, because of the way she felt about Lep, intimacy with Jeff was hard to imagine. It was nuts, she never thought she could have felt this way, but there it was. Lep had gone out of his way to follow her to protect her from Tony after school. Lep had taken a big risk by doing that. No other boy she knew had that kind of courage. He had held her and comforted her in his hard, warm, wiry arms. She wanted him to hold her again.

And he had told her about Tony giving him test answers. That was her ace in the hole—it was what could really get *both* Tony and Warren. But it was such a sacrifice for Lep! How would he ever graduate *without* cheating? She understood why he had to cheat.

She would have to help him, that was all. They would make the time. She would tutor him for real. She would do anything she had to do. And if they were incredibly lucky, and things worked out the way she was fantasizing, maybe the test wouldn't matter so much anymore.

Tony did not appear the whole way to school.

Luckily Jeff always sat with his own group of guys at lunch, so she could eat with Lep. She wanted to hold hands with him, she wanted to kiss him, but not in the school cafeteria.

She felt she no longer had to be careful of what she said to him. He had given his secret away to her. He knew what she wanted to do to Tony and Warren. He was on her side. "Warren's daughter called our house yesterday," she told him. "She didn't say who she was, but I'm sure it was her."

"Why she do that?" Lep leaned forward. She

loved how his black, black hair, crew cut, framed his dark face.

"She wanted to talk to my father. My guess is that she's afraid he's going to tell her father that we saw her with Tony on his motorcycle. Don't you think she'd be afraid of that?"

Lep nodded vehemently. "Make big, big problem for Tony. Then she never see him again. And I think she like to see him."

"What's she like? Did you ever meet her?"

He laughed, shaking his head. "Meet her? You think anybody introduce *me* to *her*? But I see her one time when she come to Grand Diamond. And I watch her. She don't know I watching her." He seemed pleased by that.

"So what was she like?"

"Like rich people." He winked, and laughed again. "She look down on everybody. She kind of person who talk about 'Third World,' and what she buy there."

She could tell by the sound of his voice that he hated that term, "Third World." She wished she had never used it, not even with her father.

"But she nice to Tony," Lep said, his smile mocking. "*Very* nice to Tony. What is word? She . . . uh . . . *flirt* with Tony."

That made Ann disgusted. This girl had a crush on the man who wanted to kill her? "What do you think would happen if her father found out about her and Tony?"

Lep's expression changed. He pressed his lips together for a moment. Then he sighed. "Tony go. Many problem for everybody. And no more test answers."

"Then we'll have to wait." Now Ann leaned forward. "You saved the answers he gave you already, right?"

He nodded.

"Can you bring them to school?"

"Yes," he said.

"Yesterday you said . . ." She was hesitant about this, but he *had* mentioned it, after all. "You said they made you do other things to get XCAS answers. Can you tell me what you did?"

He seemed like he was about to close up again, his eyes downcast. Then he looked up into her eyes.

"Woman live in building, no money . . . like everybody live there—nobody there pass XCAS. Woman work as waitress." He spoke very haltingly, as if reluctant to admit what had happened. "Tony tell me many time she always late for pay rent. She always complain to Tony if light don't work or toilet don't flush. She have four-year-old little girl who have to stay alone sometime when she work. Tony don't like her. Want her to move out of building. So Tony tell me . . ."

He looked down again.

She took his hand. She didn't care if anybody saw. "Lep, don't worry. You know you can trust me. And this might be important. We want to stop them."

He squeezed her hand. "Tony want me to make bad electric in room. Make it dangerous so maybe fire start when little girl alone there. To scare mother, make her move away. He tell me he give me XCAS answers if I do that. First time he say he give me XCAS answers. I want to finish high school, have better life. Have to pass XCAS. So I do it." He said the last words very quickly, and pulled his hand away, looking down again.

How could she make him understand she didn't think he was a bad person for doing that? It was XCAS—and the corruption of Tony and Warren—that was behind it all, not anything about Lep. "What happened to the little girl?"

"Very lucky. Spark come from fan when mother is home. Curtain start to burn. Mother scared. She and little girl move away. Better for her to live someplace where no Tony."

"Lep. I understand why you did that. I know you didn't want to. But you had no choice. If you told Tony you wouldn't do that, what would he do?"

"Fire me from job I need and get somebody else to do it for little money. And not give me any XCAS answers. Throw *us* out of building. Then my sister very mad at me. And no hope to finish high school for better life."

"Like I said, you had no choice," Ann told him. "I know you're a good person—you took a big risk to follow me home from school because you were worried about Tony hurting me. But if we don't do *something* to try to stop them, they'll make you do more things like that."

He looked at her, hard. "Tony already make me do more. Make me loosen balcony railing in apartment with four kids. Man I don't like, treat me like dirt, also late for rent. He make me break his toilet so everything come up and flood his room. Then make me clean up the mess. He make me clean up mess from toilet a *lot*." He paused. "Tony find me at prison school last year, where they put me after first time I take XCAS. I think they have special question on test to find people they think dangerous to country. Very bad there. Only one bathroom for many people. Sleep in room with many people, some of them dangerous. Fighting. Other things . . . Very glad Tony take me out. I do almost anything to get out of there."

"My God," Ann murmured. "I bet *curity* looks at the test. Especially the tests taken by foreign students."

"I think Warren find Tony at that prison school too, years ago," Lep said. "Other people too. I think he have many people working for him, doing bad things, so he don't do them himself, and get caught. Grand Diamond only very small thing for Mr. Warren. Oil and test more important for him. And corruption there too. You really think we can stop it?"

She nodded, very firmly and confidently. "Now that I know about Tony giving you the test answers, and what he makes you do for them. Now that Tony shot at me. You remember the license number of that bike he was riding?"

"G571."

"What about the card that man gave you? The man who saw Tony shoot at me? Do you still have it? Did you look at it?"

He reached into his pants pocket and pulled out the card. "I don't read it yet," he said, holding it up to his eyes. "Frank Gilroy," he read slowly. "Investigative Re . . . Reporter. NBS News."

"Wait a minute," she said. "Let me see it."

He handed it to her. She read it quickly. "I don't believe this!" she said, very excited now. "This guy is a *newsman*! And he saw Tony shoot at me. And he wanted to interview us!" How could such good luck be possible? "It's a sign," she said. "A sign that we're doing the right thing, on the right track. I want to see those test answers. Bring them tomorrow. And you don't have to worry about me. Jeff is walking with me now—for the rest of the week, anyway. Tomorrow's Friday and I want to see the test answers then."

The bell screamed and they got up. They both had other classes to go to before English.

Ann was sure Lep hadn't done the assignment about finding out what technology they had in 1909. He had to work, and he had no computer access. She hadn't done much either, because she had still been shaken up by Tony shooting at her. She had stayed in her room, pretending to work at the computer, though, not wanting her parents to know anything unusual had happened. She didn't think it really mattered that she hadn't done the assignment, because Ms. Summers hadn't asked for anything to be handed in. They were going to have a discussion, and she could participate in that, and maybe even Lep, like he had yesterday. English was pretty amazing now, with Ms. Summers. Even after what had happened with Tony, Ann was still curious about what the class was going to be like.

It still felt unfamiliar to sit in a circle. And, as if by habit, everyone took their same seats, Ann next to Lep. They knew Ms. Summers didn't care what order they sat in, but it was too much of a habit to break in a day or two. Anyway, it might help her to remember their names if they stayed in the same places. Unlike Wells, Ms. Summers thought it was important to call them by name.

Ann hoped Wells was going to be sick forever. She got out the little recorder she used to tape some of her classes. It helped remind her of details in long lectures. But this time she used it because she knew she would want to relive this exciting class.

"So," Ms. Summers said. "What technology did they have in 1909? We'll start with that, and then try to figure out what could have made this writer so afraid of it."

Keith raised his hand first. Ms. Summers consulted her paper. "Yes, Keith," she said.

"They had cars. And Henry Ford invented mass production," he said.

A girl named Nina raised her hand and when Ms. Summers found out her name, Nina said, "The Wright brothers made their first airplane flight before 1909. And in 1907 somebody invented the first piloted helicopter."

It turned out they had zeppelins, escalators, vacuum cleaners, air conditioners, and even movies. The other students had done their homework well.

"Now . . . can anybody think what might have made this writer see technology as dangerous?"

For a long moment, nobody moved. Then, to Ann's great surprise, Lep slowly raised his hand. What could he have thought of?

"Well, if they just start having cars then, maybe roads not so good. Maybe have car accident," he said.

Along with everything else great about him, Lep was really smart too, Ann thought. She had been in English class with him since the beginning of the year, and she never knew he was smart until *now*, in this very different kind of English class.

"You're absolutely right, Lep," Ms. Summers said. "Cars were very different then, not as safe. They shared the roads with horse-drawn carriages, and there *were* accidents in which people got injured in horrible new ways. I think the writer of this story, E. M. Forster, might have been thinking about that." She paused. "What else? What about the fact that every room in the earth is exactly alike? Where could he have gotten that idea?"

Ann remembered what Keith had said. She raised her hand. "Mass production," she said.

"Very good!" Ms. Summers beamed at her. "Probably most people thought mass production was wonderful—they could make complicated things like cars so quickly and cheaply. But what would it seem like to a different kind of person, who was used to most things being made by hand?"

Lep raised his hand again. "In Thailand," he said shyly, "in countryside, everybody make their own house. Every house different. Here, many apartment all the same. Maybe that writer, he think, life not as . . ." He shrugged, as if searching for a word. "He think life not as—lovely as before, because everything same."

Ann felt as if Ms. Summers wanted to clap. Ann did too. Lep had thought of that himself, and none of the other students had. "I'm positive that mass production was a big factor in that story, and for that very reason," Ms. Summers said. "He keeps stressing how everything is exactly the same, all over the world, and how much richness and culture is missing from everyone's life because of that." She leaned forward in her chair. "You know, you kids really know how to think. I bet you never really had to . . . well, never mind."

Mass production; people listening to radios and watching movies instead of talking directly to each other and spending their time outside; car accidents—all had contributed to the story, even before World War I. Ann had never been in a class like this before. Again, she wondered where they had found Ms. Summers—and how long they would let her continue.

Their assignment for tonight was to look at the story again and think about the characters—why they were the way they were. Not just Vashti and Kuno, but also some of the people Vashti had seen on the airship, and especially the lecturers who worshipped the Machine. Ann hoped she could relax enough about the situation with Tony to be able to think about it a little. She packed up her recorder and headed to her next class.

Jeff walked her home again. This time he held her

hand. He was rough about it, not gentle like Lep. She didn't want him to. But what choice did she have? And if she was holding hands with him she probably was safer from Tony. Again, Tony did not appear. And again, Jeff urged her to drop by on Saturday night.

The next day at lunch Lep gave her the papers Tony had given him. She looked at them quickly—there wouldn't be much time before the bell rang. Some of them were the answers to the English paragraphs—that was obviously how Lep had worked his way up so quickly to the middle of Wells's class from the bottom. But others were different. They were questions and answers Ann had never seen before, not just English, but math and social studies too. "What are these?" she asked Lep. "I never saw them."

"Tony say very important. Not just for practice. For big test, to graduate."

Ann felt the excitement and danger in her gut. "For the *big* XCAS? The *real* XCAS, that you can't graduate unless you pass it?"

"That what he say."

Ann put them carefully into her bag. "It's like they're worth a million dollars," she murmured.

"A billion," Lep said, and laughed his throaty chuckle.

"Do you know the name of that woman who was forced to leave the building, the one with the four-year-old daughter?"

"I don't know her name, but somebody in building know it."

"Do you think they'll know where she went? How to find her? *She'd* like to get Tony and Warren in trouble too, I bet."

Lep looked uncomfortable. "But . . . it is me who make the dangerous electric."

"It was Tony and Warren who *made* you do it so you could graduate from high school. Nobody will blame you."

The bell screamed.

15

After the awful girl had hung up on her, and Elise had gotten rid of that big fattening dinner, she went online again. She zoomed down on the pathetic little apartment building where the Forrest family lived. She went to another site and found the closest public school, and back to the map again. She found the school. How did the girl get there? Did she take the bus, ride in a car, or walk? Elise thought of the comfort of her copter, and that made her a little less angry.

But that family still had to be kept quiet. How was she going to do it?

Tony.

Maybe she and Tony could do it together! Tony had more to worry about from them than she did. He could lose his job because that family had seen him with Elise. Tony was the whole reason she wanted to shut them up.

And she and Tony could spend more time together while they were doing whatever he thought they should do. Should she call him now?

She felt a little hesitant. But then she told herself, *You're the boss's daughter.* And the last time she called him it had worked out fine. She found him on her phone and pressed the call key.

She got a recorded message. She didn't leave a message herself—she was afraid somebody else might hear it. Why hadn't he answered his phone? Was he spending time with some other girl, with the phone turned off?

He couldn't know anybody else as young, or as rich, or as pivotal to his life as she was. She would keep calling. She'd get him soon. She was plagued with jealousy.

She called him again the next day, Thursday, before dinner. "Grand Diamond Management," he said.

"Hi, Tony, it's Elise. I had such a great time the other day."

"Oh! So did I." He always seemed a little startled when she called. "Ah, where are you calling from?"

"From home. But my parents aren't here," she lied. "Listen, I have something important to talk to you about."

"What?" He sounded a little impatient. But why should he be impatient with *her*? Because of that man seeing them together, of course! He was worried about his job now. He might never want to go out with her again!

"That guy who worked as a health aide or something, Forrest. And his wife and daughter and son. All of them seeing us together. We've got to make sure they keep their mouths shut."

There was dead silence at the other end of the phone. Should she say something? Should she wait to get his reaction?

"Tony?" she said tentatively. "Shouldn't we—"

"*I've* got to make sure," Tony said coldly. "You'd better keep out of it."

"But . . ." She was hurt. "Isn't there something

I could do to . . . to help? I know where they live. I know what school—"

"I told you to keep out of it," he said. "I can take care of it." And he hung up.

Elise was stunned. Two people hanging up on her, that girl and now Tony! People never hung up on her. And now that this had happened, she realized the terrible blunder she had made. How could she be so stupid? Reminding Tony they had been seen together would only drive him away from her. Now he definitely wouldn't want to go out with her again. And it was all her own fault.

And the fault of that girl.

She seethed at the thought of her. Her and her grubby, interfering father. Whatever Tony said, she would prove she cared about him. She could get them. Then Tony would go out with her again. Everything was on her side. She had money. She had a copter at her disposal. The Forrests had nothing.

She just had to figure out a way to do it without her father knowing anything about it. He was the impediment.

And at dinner that night her father said, "We're

going away tomorrow, Friday. Dinner at the White House Saturday night, and I have some consulting with the administration. We won't be back until Sunday. But of course the entire staff will be here, and security, so I'm not worried about you getting into trouble."

"Of course not, Daddy," she said demurely. But she was already planning. Could she bribe the copter driver to silence? There was plenty of money in her bank account, and she could always say she had spent it on clothes—shoes were a big expense her father allowed; he wanted to be proud of the way she dressed.

Could she trust the copter driver, Henry? That was the question. It was so irritating the way everybody had to tiptoe around her father instead of just doing what *she* wanted! But even if she could get the copter to go where she wanted, where could she go to find that family? There would be no place to land anywhere in their neighborhood—she was sure nobody where they lived had the money. But somehow, she had to find her and make sure she and her father kept their mouths shut, and that Tony knew she had done it too. But how? How . . .

At the computer after dinner she zoomed in closer than before on the girl's school. And there *was* a tarmac for copters there! Probably for curity purposes; public schools had big crime problems. And her school always got out earlier than other schools on Fridays, to make it easier for all the students who didn't have copters. And maybe she could bring one of her friends along too, to make it less suspicious to Henry. She could make up some event happening at this public school that she and her friend wanted to attend and show off to the public school kids. That would seem ordinary to Henry. And she could bribe him with something to be quiet about it.

She could just pretend to be friendly with the Forrest girl and get her into the copter with them. And then they could scare the hell out of her.

She got on the phone to start making the arrangements for Friday.

In English on Friday they talked about the characters in the story, why Vashti and the others were slaves of the Machine, why they worshipped it like a god. And why Kuno was different. It was only about a million times more interesting than anything that had ever happened in Wells's class.

Vashti and almost everyone else in that world were pale, inert lumps of flesh, like toadstools. They never moved; if they dropped something, the floor of their cell picked it up for them. When Vashti had boarded the airship a man had dropped the precious Book of the Machine on the ramp, but it was too much trouble for him to bend over and pick it up, even though it was like the Bible to them, and people had just trod over it.

Vashti's son, Kuno, was the only one who exercised, who walked up and down the tunnels and swung from metal beams to try to get strong enough to find his own way to climb out. He hated being confined. His mother thought he was crazy.

But Ann was distracted, thinking about the incriminating documents Lep had given her at lunch. She had them now, safely in her possession. And they were just as incriminating to Warren and Tony as anyone could hope.

But what, exactly, was she going to do with them?

She couldn't go straight to the reporter. Why would he believe a couple of kids? She needed an authority figure to help. Who? Everybody permanently at the school, even the teachers who probably hated it, was so trapped by XCAS that they wouldn't be happy about this evidence of corruption behind it. Who could she show Lep's papers to who would *want* to get Warren to stop making the test, and get Tony in big trouble for giving away the answers?

And then the obvious answer came to her: Ms. Summers.

There was not enough time between classes. She would have to arrange to meet with Ms. Summers after school. She would have to get Jeff to wait for her, somewhere else. He would do it if she could use her visit to his house when his parents were away as a bribe. She still didn't know what she was going to do about Saturday night. How could she bribe him and then get out of it?

It would be even better if Lep could be there with Ms. Summers too, to explain in his own words why they had given the test answers to him and what they had made him do to get them. Ms. Summers did seem to like both Ann and Lep. But Lep would have to hurry after to get to work.

Unless Tony was away from the building, waiting for her again. That was a distinct possibility. She felt her pulse pick up in fear.

Did she dare tell Ms. Summers about Tony trying to kill her? Was that too much to lay on a substitute, to drag her into this mess—a substitute as nice as Ms. Summers?

But who else at the school was she going to tell? Who else could she trust? Now that she thought about it, it was very likely that the principal, or anybody else, might *destroy* the evidence. After all, who would want to make problems about the all-important test? The principal, for instance, would get in trouble with the superintendent, and the superintendent would get in trouble with the governor. The governor, after all, would want to be on good terms with the federal administration, and the administration was behind the test 100 percent. It would not be good for him politically to bring forth evidence that the test was a sham and a cheat.

Ann and Lep couldn't do it on their own; they were merely students, at the very bottom of the heap. They needed somebody with a tiny bit of authority. Ms. Summers didn't have much. But she had more than they did.

After class she signaled to Lep to approach the teacher with her. "Excuse me, Ms. Summers," she said. "Lep and I have something very important to talk to you about after school—something about the test."

Ms. Summers frowned. "I hope you're not going to complain about how I'm not preparing you adequately for that thing, because I'm—"

"No, no!" Ann vehemently shook her head. "Maybe some of the other students feel that way, but not us. What we want to talk to you about is exactly the opposite of that. In fact, you're the only person at the whole school who we *can* talk to about this." She turned to Lep. "I hope you can be here too, Lep, even if it might make you a little bit late for work."

Ms. Summers's face softened. "Oh, that's right. You have to work after school, Lep. Even with all the extra studying you have to do to keep up with the students from America. I hope you realize how bright you are, and that you have the potential to be an excellent student—in a real school, that is."

Lep grinned. He loved the praise. "I will be here after school," he said.

Ann was too distracted to concentrate during the rest of her classes. What would Ms. Summers do about the test answers? She was a good person and she obviously didn't like the test. But what was in it for her to go so actively against the test? Nothing.

Her involvement could sabotage any serious career plans.

But she was their only hope at the school.

After school she told Jeff she had something important to do and would he mind waiting a few minutes? When he grumbled, she mentioned that she was free Saturday night and he smiled and said he would wait outside. She met Lep in front of the English classroom. They squeezed their hands together briefly, then went in.

Ms. Summers looked up from the papers she was studying and shook her head. "You poor kids, having to spend all your time on this cr—I mean on this pointless stuff. I knew about it, of course, but if I'd known more I might not have . . . Well, anyway, what's on your minds?"

"Nobody likes the test," Ann said. "The kids all hate it, and I think a lot of the teachers do too, though they won't admit it to us. It's the administrators who like it because it makes everything easier for them—they know how to pigeonhole us in a snap. Well, we have some incriminating evidence about the test. Lep gave it to me."

Ms. Summers leaned forward with interest. "What could you possibly have that could be incriminating about that god-awful thing?"

"Tell her, Lep."

Lep started off haltingly, but as he got more into the story he became more eloquent in his weird way. Ms. Summers's eyes widened when he said he lived in a building owned by the publisher of the test. And when he told her how they had first given him test answers to bribe him to do something criminal and dangerous, her mouth literally fell open.

"The man who publishes the test did that?" she said in disbelief.

"Owner of company. I know because of—how you say it, Ann?"

"The logo of his group of companies is on the test," Ann said. "He's very close to the president."

When Lep finished telling about the dangerous and disgusting things they made him do for test answers, she told about her father helping other people in the same building, and how Tony got rid of him by threatening her. "And on Wednesday Tony actually shot at me," she said. "Now I'm terrified every time I have to go back and forth to school. This man saw it happen and offered to help." She let her look at the card. "We're afraid the principal or the superintendent or somebody like that might not want to listen, might hush it all up." She shrugged. "And who are *we* to go against *them*?"

"A reporter?" Ms. Summers said, sounding very interested. "This could be big news. You're right that you two can't do it by yourselves. You could use some publicity, even just as protection. I mean, what you're trying to do is very dangerous, going against people like that killer and his boss . . ."

"I tell her that," Lep put in.

"Yes. And it will mean losing your source of test answers too, Lep," Ms. Summers said softly. "And *you'd* probably be in just as much danger as Ann then. I'm not sure how to take the first step myself. Let's see what this reporter has to say. I've had some experience with them. I'm surprised he wasn't more aggressive, after what he saw. Do you have a cell phone? Call him now."

Ann reached into her handbag and pulled out her cell phone. Her parents had pounded it into her that she was only supposed to use it for emergencies. But if this wasn't an emergency, then what was? She dialed the number on the card.

And got a message. "Frank Gilroy here. Out of town on assignment. Tell me your business and your number and I'll try to call you back on Monday."

She was so disappointed she didn't know what to say for a moment. But she probably didn't have much time. "This is Ann Forrest, the girl you saw being shot at this week by a guy on a motorcycle. I want to tell you the whole story. It's big news. Business tycoon Frederick Warren is behind it." She gave him her cell phone number, even though she knew it would appear automatically.

"I can't reach him until Monday," she told them when she hung up. "If he doesn't call me, I'll have to call him back."

"It was smart of you to mention Warren." Ms. Summers nodded approvingly. "He'll know there's a real story there. Here's my cell phone number. Call if anything comes up."

They both nodded glumly. They both had their own reasons for not looking forward to the weekend.

Ann and Lep held hands briefly again outside the classroom. Then Lep went out the back door and Ann went out in front to meet Jeff.

She noticed the copter on the tarmac right away. A copter there almost always meant some kind of trouble, either criminal or medical, but there had been no alarm bells today. There were two unfamiliar girls standing at the edge of the group of students, two exceedingly well-dressed and well-groomed girls, better dressed than almost anybody at Ann's school. And then Ann recognized one of them—the girl they had seen with Tony, Warren's daughter. What was *she* doing here?

Unexpectedly the girl waved and smiled at Ann the moment she saw her. Ann lifted her hand and waved tentatively. What on earth was going on?

Jeff looked back and forth between them, mystified. "You *know* those girls?" he whispered to Ann. "Who are they?"

What could she say? That one of them was the daughter of the man who owned the company that published the test? Whose hit man was the real reason she wanted Jeff to walk with her, because he had tried to kill her?

The two girls strolled over to them, erect and self-confident. Why was the Warren girl acting so friendly? She had accused Ann's father of not minding his own business, and Ann had called *her* father a goon and hung up on her. She didn't look like the kind of person who would want to apologize and make up and be friends. Not with somebody like Ann.

Unless she wanted to frighten her, like Tony was doing, but in her own way. It sure *was* a good thing Jeff was with her. And it was also lucky that Lep had gone out the back door—she might recognize him, and if she saw him with Ann, he'd get in trouble too.

"Hi, I'm Elise," she said to Ann. "And this is Becky. Sorry we got started off on the wrong foot the other night. I wanted to make up for it. Would you—and your friend"—she smiled at Jeff— "like to go for a spin in my copter?"

It was all Jeff could do not to let his mouth drop open. He couldn't possibly think this rich girl was prettier than Ann, because she wasn't. But she had all the money it took to make herself look as stunning as possible.

And had Jeff ever been in a copter before? Ann doubted it. She hadn't.

"A ride in a copter?" Jeff said in awe. He turned excitedly to Ann. "Hey, cool! Let's go."

Ann didn't know what to say. What, exactly, was behind this? It couldn't possibly be friendliness. Ann knew this girl's goal was to shut Ann's family up. Would it be safe riding in her copter?

Ann had never been in one before, but she knew something about them. She could tell from the size of the copter that it was only a four-seater, one seat for the pilot. And with the three girls and Jeff, there would be five people in it. "Thanks," Ann said, trying to sound civil. "But . . . is there room for all of us? It looks like a four-seater."

Elise shrugged. "No problem. We do it all the time."

"Come on, Ann," Jeff said impatiently. "Let's go. It's Friday. It won't matter if we get home late."

"No," Ann said firmly.

Jeff looked like he wanted to punch her. So did Elise.

"Then you and I have to have a little chat. Alone," Elise said.

Elise had gotten up early that morning,
before her father came down to breakfast, and poured
a hefty amount of vodka into a plastic mineral water
bottle. She knew that Henry, her copter pilot, liked
to drink, though as far as she knew he had never done
it while flying the copter before. But this, and some
cash, would really shut him up.

Henry held the copter door open for her. Before
she climbed in she said, "You know school gets out
early on Friday, Henry. So I'm not going to go straight
home today. A friend and I are going to another school
to meet some friends and take them for a ride."

"Very good, Miss Warren," Henry said, but

he looked puzzled. He knew her father didn't like passengers because more weight ate up more gas.

"It's OK about the gas," she said. "I'll deal with my father if he notices." She climbed in and Henry shut the door carefully behind her. She had always thought it was too bad that Henry wasn't good-looking. But now that she almost had Tony, it didn't matter anymore.

"Oh, and I'd just as soon nobody found out about it," she said, before she sat down, as he was climbing into the pilot's seat in front. "My parents will have left for D.C. before we get back anyway, and they're not coming home until Sunday. And I can make it worth your while." She handed him fifty dollars and the bottle. "Take a smell of this water. I think you'll like it." She had overheard her parents talking about how much he liked to drink on his time off, and wondering how safe he really was.

Henry obediently unscrewed the bottle cap and took a sniff. Then he looked back at her, startled. "But . . . but you know I can't touch this stuff when I'm working," he protested.

"You can do whatever you want as far as I'm

concerned," Elise said, settling into her seat and snapping on the belts. "Nobody's going to know anything about this little trip anyway."

And it had worked. She could smell the alcohol on his breath when he held the door open for her and Becky after school. And he was flying differently, a little wobbly on the takeoff. She laughed inwardly. This sure would keep him quiet about the whole thing. And it was exciting too, like riding on Tony's motorcycle without a helmet.

She loved the bewildered look on the Forrest girl's face when she saw her out in front of her school. She really was pretty. But her clothes were obviously from a discount store, a cheap denim skirt and a cotton blouse cut a little low. Elise couldn't help resenting that she obviously didn't need a padded bra the way Elise did. But Elise was so much more in control of everything that she told herself there was no need for her to be bothered about that. The boy she was with was surprisingly cute too. Elise could get him away from her with a snap of her fingers if she wanted. But why should she want him, when there was Tony?

She was lying about ever squeezing five people

into the copter, but the boy might as well come along too, just for the hell of it, if Henry would allow it. The boy being there wouldn't interfere with her plans. Elise had to be discreet with the Forrest girl. This girl had a temper and she had guts. Elise would play it cool with her from now on.

And then she refused to get into the copter. The boy she was with looked as angry with her as Elise was.

"Then you and I have to have a little chat. Alone," Elise said, seething.

"Gladly," the girl said. "I've been looking forward to this."

Elise was shocked, and not pleased. This girl was not afraid of her, like everybody else was. Was she going to be able to persuade her of anything?

"Where can we go to be alone?" Elise asked her.

"Out in back of the school. There won't be anybody there now." She turned to the boy. "Jeff, would you mind waiting just for a few minutes more?"

The boy frowned at her—he had really wanted to ride in the copter. But he said, "OK, Ann, sure. Whatever you want."

The boy must want something from her, otherwise he would have gotten angry and refused to wait. Elise could guess what it was. But she didn't care about that. Now she knew her name was Ann, which would make their conversation easier.

"Come on," Ann said to Elise. "This way." And they walked away from the others, around the side of the building.

As soon as they were out of earshot of the others, Ann said, "You're terrified my father's going to tell your father we saw you with Tony, aren't you?"

"Oh, shut up!" Elise said, unable for the moment to think of anything else.

"So what did you want to tell me?" Ann asked her, reaching into her bag for a moment.

"You and your busybody father know . . . something I don't want anybody else to know. And nobody's going to find out."

Ann laughed. How could she possibly laugh? "What makes you think you can threaten me? I'm sure not going to keep it a secret that my whole family saw you with Tony on his motorcycle." Ann smiled at her wickedly. "Did you know that your precious boyfriend shot at me the other day? Did he tell you *that*?"

No, Elise didn't know Tony had done that stupid thing. Now Ann had even more evidence against him. How *could* she shut this horrible girl up? She had never imagined she'd be so difficult. She hadn't planned any specific threats; she hadn't thought she'd need them.

And then she remembered how her father recruited people. He didn't know she knew about it, but she had eavesdropped enough to be sure. The place where he found young criminals to do his dirty work for him in many of his businesses, so that if anybody got caught it would be them, not him. "I have connections with a top-security juvenile detention center downtown," Elise said. "Would you like to leave your lovely school and go and live there for a few years?"

They were behind the school now, and Ann had been right; there was nobody else around. "Yeah, I know all about that," Ann said, surprising Elise yet again. "Just try it, and the whole world will know about how your father finds his goons."

Elise stamped her foot. "Oh, shut up!" she said

again. She had no idea this little twit was going to be so tough. What *could* she threaten her with, that would really scare her?

"No! *You* shut up!" Ann fired back at her.

"How dare you!" Elise shrieked, and slapped her face.

Ann slammed her fist into Elise's perfectly sculpted nose. Elise actually heard something crack, and she screamed at the pain of it. And now blood was pouring out. How could this creature possibly be getting the better of her?

Ann pulled a package of tissues out of her bag and handed it to Elise. "Here. Be grateful I have these," she said.

Elise was dying to throttle her, but now she didn't dare. Ann obviously had a lot of practice fighting physically, and Elise didn't. What on earth was she going to do? She held a wad of tissues up to her damaged nose, on the verge of tears.

And then she thought of it. The test.

For someone like Ann, everything depended on the test. The test ruled. "Did you know that my father owns the company that publishes XCAS?

The test that people like you have to pass in order to graduate?" Elise said thickly, because of the blood. Could her expensive nose be broken? It was all she could do not to burst into tears. But she was able to hold them back. She had too much pride to cry in front of this poor little slob.

"Of course I know all about Replico and your father and XCAS. Do you think I'm a dope?" Ann said.

Why did she know so much? But at least it was good in that Elise didn't have to prove it to her. She didn't know if what she was about to say was true, but Ann wouldn't know that either. And she wanted to get this girl really bad now. "Well, the people at Replico treat me like royalty. They'll do anything I want them to," Elise said. "The people who run the computers that grade the test work there too. I can make sure you don't pass it, and you'll never graduate; they can make it so the computers automatically flunk anyone with your name. I can give them bonuses for failing a nothing little person like you, even if you do happen to pass. And then you'll be stuck in your miserable little life in the traffic forever. Like those people in the buildings my father owns."

For some reason Ann clutched more tightly at her pathetic denim bag, which was more frayed than her skirt. "Oh, really?" she said conversationally. "What a very interesting thing for you to say. I'll have to remember that."

"You better remember it," Elise said vehemently. The blood finally seemed to be stopping. "Because if my father, or anybody else, hears one word about me and Tony, or whatever you claim Tony did to you— then you're not going to pass. You got that?"

"I got it," Ann said, almost cheerfully. "And like I said, I'll remember it. So there's no need for you to worry. I know how to keep my mouth shut. I intend on passing the test, no matter what."

"Good," Elise said, beginning to calm down. The test had such all-consuming importance that Ann finally seemed to be bending to her will. The way she had expected her to from the beginning. Of course Ann wasn't going to act contrite or anything. That wasn't her way. But it was clear that she understood the power of the test—and that Elise wielded that power.

"OK. I'm glad we agree." She had to get home and take care of her nose. If it really was broken and she had to go to the doctor, how would she explain that to her father? One more horrible thing she hadn't anticipated. She was about to threaten to sue Ann if she had seriously hurt her, but stopped herself in time. Ann had agreed to be quiet. She didn't want to do anything to change that.

They made it silently back to the front of the school, both thinking hard. That was good. Elise had finally gotten through to this tough little thing. She couldn't wait to tell Tony that they were safe from now on.

18

Ann tried to be evasive with Jeff on the way home. They were holding hands, which she didn't like, but she didn't know how to refuse without making him angry. Of course he was curious about what had happened to Elise, and who she was, and how Ann knew her. She didn't want to tell him about Tony threatening her and shooting at her. She didn't want the whole school to know about that—yet. "My father used to work in a building her rich father owns," she told him. "My father had to stop working there because he got in trouble for helping the people too much." She shrugged. "Rich people are like that. So now her whole family hates my family. That's why we had a fight, and that's why I didn't want to ride in her copter."

Jeff looked confused. But he didn't press her to say more, for the same reason he had waited for her after school. "I can't wait for tomorrow night," he said eagerly.

Holding Jeff's hand was nothing like holding hands with Lep; the feeling wasn't there.

"We can drink," Jeff went on enthusiastically. "My parents won't notice if anything is missing. And I have some other stuff too. You *are* coming, aren't you? You *have* to come!"

She knew what going over there without anybody else would mean, and she didn't want that with Jeff, cute and popular as he was. She especially didn't want it now, because of the way she felt about Lep—a new kind of tenderness she had never felt about any boy before. She and Lep shared so much now—Grand Diamond, fighting the test with Ms. Summers and loving her class, the fear of Tony, and how wonderfully comforting Lep had been after the shooting. Things she didn't share with Jeff, who was definitely becoming a drag.

But what excuse could she use? Her parents? But

Jeff already knew they were free with her about what she did on weekends; she and Jeff had been at the same parties.

Was he really serious about her, the way she knew Lep would be if he believed it were possible? Or was he just interested in fooling around, like most boys? "I still haven't checked with my parents," she said lamely.

"You wouldn't tell them my parents aren't going to be there?" Jeff said quickly, sounding worried.

"No, no," she said. "I just have to make sure it's OK with them."

Jeff frowned and let go of her hand, and she felt guilty. "I'll call you tomorrow morning," he said, not sounding so friendly anymore. And that seemed to her to be more evidence that he didn't really care about her, the way Lep did.

On Saturday morning, she had an idea. The big question was, would she be safe walking to and from school without Jeff? She had to take that risk. She called him after breakfast.

"Oh, hi," he said, sounding half grateful and half worried. "I was just going to call you."

"Well, I told my parents I had a fight with that girl, Elise. And they're so mad at me they grounded me for the rest of the weekend."

"Grounded you?" He sounded angry. "Why? It wasn't *your* fault she was mad at you."

"Yeah, but they didn't like it that I had a fight with a girl whose father is so rich and famous and important. They keep telling me I need to learn how to control my temper. They think they're teaching me a lesson. I'm sorry, Jeff. It's just not possible this weekend."

"But I don't know when my parents are going to go away again!" he said, raising his voice.

"I can't do anything about that," she said.

"Thanks for nothing!" Jeff said angrily, and hung up.

Now she just felt relieved, without a trace of guilt. Jeff could put on a show of being nice, but underneath he was just like so many other guys, only after how much he could get. The opposite of Lep.

Of course, now Jeff would be telling everybody nasty things about her, how she was just a big tease and stuff like that. But she didn't care anymore. The people he would tell these things to weren't the people who mattered to her now. And anyway, they would all see through him and know he was only saying it because she had turned him down. She didn't worry about it.

Instead, she thought about Lep for the whole weekend. What was happening to him? What was Tony putting him through? For once, she couldn't wait until Monday.

It was the middle of May now, testing for real would be starting very soon, but it was still dark early on Monday morning when she started off for school, alone for the first time since the day Tony had shot at her. If she made it OK this one last time, she might be safe from now on, if the reporter would get involved. She was going to call the reporter again today, and if he was willing to see her she was hoping like crazy that Lep would be able to go with her, and not have to rush back to work.

She took a different route than usual, and she was more alert than ever. It gradually began to get light. There was no motorcycle with the Replico logo, no driver in a studded leather jacket, no motorcycle with that other license number either. And finally the school came into sight. She had made it.

She did feel a slight chill when she said hello to some of her friends. Jeff must have been very busy all weekend IM-ing and texting about her to everybody he could think of. So what? What she was looking forward to was lunch with Lep, and telling him what had happened with Elise.

Lep was already at the table waiting for her, alone. For some reason she felt like crying when she saw him. She hurried over to him and put down her tray and he stood up and they hugged briefly. It didn't matter if anybody saw.

He was wearing the Replico T-shirt. "Good shirt to be wearing today," Ann told him, hoping the reporter would agree to see her and that Lep would come too.

She told him everything that had happened, especially about how Elise had threatened to put her in a detention center and make sure she didn't pass XCAS if anybody found out about her and Tony.

"She scared of you, right?" he asked her, and smiled.

"It sure seemed like it."

"She so rich, but *you* in control," he said, sounding very pleased.

"And I recorded it all too," she told him.

He held her hand to his cheek and beamed.

Tony had to be worried that she or her father might tell Warren about him and Elise. He couldn't stand to lose the power he had in that building, and his association with someone as important as Warren. That's why he had tried to shoot her. Naturally Tony took his anxiety out on Lep, who had spent the weekend working long hours doing exhausting and sickening—and unnecessary—chores. He looked it, thinner than ever, with big circles around his eyes.

"Of course you would end up being Tony's scapegoat," Ann said.

"But another thing I worry about very much."

"What?" Ann leaned forward.

"I hope Wells never come back. I hope Ms. Summers still there to help us."

That was something Ann hadn't even thought about. Now she was also terrified Ms. Summers would be gone. Yes, they had a connection with that reporter. But that was no guarantee that he would help them, no matter what he had said on the street. If he wouldn't, and there was no Ms. Summers, who would they turn to?

She grabbed Lep's hand again. "But you *will* come with me to the reporter, if he'll see us, Lep, right? Even if Tony gets mad? You're . . . you're central to everything."

He put his other hand on top of hers. "That why I wear this T-shirt. I will be there. For fighting XCAS. And for you. Tony can't do anything worse to me than he already do."

Ms. Summers was still there, thank God. When Ann and Lep went up to her after class, Ann asked her, "Do you know anything else about Mr. Wells? Like when he's coming back or anything?"

"They hired me for another week. I don't know anything about after that, except that testing for real is going to start, and I'll probably have to be part of administering it. You have to work fast. The reporter's office isn't far from here. Let's meet after school. We'll call him first, explain what happened, and head over to see him if he agrees."

After school, Ms. Summers was shocked that Elise had threatened Ann about the detention center and XCAS. She was impressed that Ann had recorded it all. "But that isn't the main issue with the reporter," she told them. "Yes, it's a good story, because her father is so famous, and you can use it to hook him. But it's not the most important part. What you need to concentrate on are the man following you, the shooting, and most importantly of all the corruption of the test, using it to force Lep to do illegal things." She sighed. "Remember, the test affects almost every student in the country. That's what you have to keep in mind, if you really want to try to change things. Are you ready to call him?"

Ann got her phone out of her bag. It had been turned off in school all day, of course, though when she turned it on she could see that no one had tried to call her. Had the reporter lost interest?

"He didn't even answer my message," Ann said. "Maybe he won't see us after all."

"Tell him about the Warren girl and he'll bite," Ms. Summers said.

19

He bit.

"I don't know if he remembered who I was or not, when I told him how he had seen Tony shoot at me," Ann said, when she clicked off the phone. "Maybe he sees shootings a lot. But when I told him about knowing Elise Warren, he got interested. He'll meet us at his office right away. It's right near where Tony shot at me."

They all walked over quickly.

Of course Lep didn't know anything about fancy offices, except for the pictures Tony had shown him of Mr. Warren's headquarters. The NBS building was fancy downstairs, with shiny metal and gleaming wood, and a huge security desk with lots of guards. They had to show their picture IDs, and a computer made name cards for them, and the guard had to call Mr. Gilroy's office so that somebody would come down to take them up.

While they waited for somebody to come, the guards asked Lep a lot of questions, more than they asked Ann and Ms. Summers. He was angry about it, but he acted innocent and naive, and pretended to be the kind of person who didn't know how to hide anything. "Mr. Gilroy wants to talk to him as much as to us," Ms. Summers put in, and she did sound a little angry.

It wasn't Mr. Gilroy who came down after ten minutes, it was a young woman not much older than Ann, though she wore a whole lot more makeup and her hair was very fancy. She seemed busy and preoccupied and not interested in them at all. Nobody said a word in the fast elevator up to the twenty-seventh floor.

It was different up here, not so fancy, narrow corridors between lots of little cubicles and busy people running around. The men wore shirtsleeves and ties and keyed into electronic gadgets as they walked, and the women were all made-up and dressed like the young woman who had brought them up. Mr. Gilroy had a real office. She left them at the door and ran off. The office was small, the desk piled with papers. There was a big computer and a lot of other electronic stuff Lep couldn't name.

Lep hadn't paid much attention to Mr. Gilroy when they met him on the street after the shooting; he was thinking only about Ann. All he remembered was that Mr. Gilroy had said he had seen the man shoot at her, and that he wanted to talk to them, and gave him his card. Now he got a good look at him. He was about the same age as Ann's father, but his hair was much neater and closely cut, and his face looked brightly polished.

"Sit down," he said, without getting up, and gestured at three chairs with plastic seats and backs in front of the desk. As they sat, Lep sensed that Ann felt almost as uncomfortable as he did. But she didn't want Mr. Gilroy to see it. Ms. Summers seemed right at home.

Mr. Gilroy sat down and checked his watch, then turned to Ann. "So that guy shot at you. What does he have to do with Warren? Do you know who he was? His face was invisible in that helmet."

"I sure do know who he is. He'd been threatening me for days before that," Ann said. She was more dressed up than usual today, in a blue dress with a collar. But the shining blonde hair falling to her shoulders was not businesslike at all, nor was her lipstick, a color between pink and purple.

Mr. Gilroy looked at the three of them with a puzzled expression. He turned to Ann and Lep. "I have to say, you two kids look pretty harmless. And—excuse me—you don't look like you'd have much for anybody to steal. What does this guy have against you?"

"Ann can tell you the whole story," Ms. Summers said.

Ann began, "My friend Lep and I are both really deep into this situation—Lep more than me. But the most important thing is—and you have to believe me—it isn't just ourselves that we're trying to protect from those people. It's every kid in the entire country who's being hurt by them."

Mr. Gilroy frowned. "What? What are you talking about?"

Ann leaned forward in her chair and nodded firmly. "Every student in this country, and that's the truth. Because what it's all about, at the bottom, is XCAS. Did you ever hear of XCAS?"

Lep could feel that Ann was holding her breath now, just as he was. This *was* the most important thing she could ask him; it was their only hope, really. And she had gotten right down to it at the very beginning.

Mr. Gilroy's eyes widened, but he still looked puzzled. He glanced at Ms. Summers. If he didn't know about XCAS, they weren't going to get a lot of help from him.

Mr. Gilroy scratched his head. "I don't get it," he said. "XCAS? That's that test, isn't it? The one my son's having so much trouble with?"

It was all Lep could do not to sigh with relief. Maybe they had a chance after all.

"The one almost *everyone* has trouble with," Ann said. "And those people who are threatening me and shooting at me, those crooks, they're the ones who are getting rich from it."

Now Mr. Gilroy was leaning forward too. "What are you trying to say? I know Warren has his fingers in a lot of pots, but I didn't know the test connection."

"The test is big news. Bigger than what happened between me and Elise Warren." Ann sat back, in control, and folded her arms across her chest. The blue dress was old, Lep could tell from the slightly frayed collar, but it was a very pretty color on her.

It also helped that Mr. Gilroy had seen Tony shoot at Ann. He already knew there was a real story here, and real danger.

Mr. Gilroy shrugged, and made a funny little twisted smile. "I'll listen to your story, because of my son and the trouble he's having with that test. And I especially want to hear what you know about the Warren girl. But I'm a busy man; we can't be leisurely about it." He checked his watch again. "I'll give you until five."

That didn't give them much time, but Ann took

advantage of it. She told him about Grand Diamond, and how her father used to work there, trying to help the poor people, and how Lep lived there and worked for the building manager, who never fixed the tenants' apartments. She told him the building was owned by Mr. Warren, who owned the company that published the test. "The test that every school district in the country has to buy from him, because the government says so." She paused. "And Warren's daughter told me she'd make sure I flunked it if I told anybody about her and the building manager."

Lep wanted to clap for Ann.

Mr. Gilroy sat back, his eyes on Ann. "So tell me the whole story," he said.

She told him about Tony threatening her, to scare her father away, because he tried to help the tenants stand up for their rights. "And that's not all Tony does," she said. She opened her bag and pulled out the test answers, and placed them on Mr. Gilroy's desk. "This is what Tony gives Lep, whose English isn't that perfect, so that he'll fix the wiring in people's apartment who he doesn't like, to make it dangerous so they'll move out. Like a woman with a four-year-old daughter who has to stay alone. Without these XCAS answers, Lep wouldn't pass, and would never graduate and have a better life."

Mr. Gilroy glanced quickly at the papers. "Yeah, yeah. So Warren's building manager bribes him with test answers. Tell me about Warren's daughter," he said, and looked at his watch.

Ann tried to bring Lep in again. "It's a coincidence that his name is an educational term. L.E.P. 'Limited English Proficiency,'" Ann said. "Our teacher—not Ms. Summers—doesn't like having L.E.P. students in his class. They bring down the average test scores, and that makes the teacher look bad."

Mr. Gilroy clucked his teeth perfunctorily, then asked Ann, "What do you have to do with Warren's daughter?"

Ann told Mr. Gilroy about her whole family seeing Mr. Warren's daughter with Tony, the man who had shot at her. It made Lep want to shout with laughter that she was telling this to a newsman. Lep added, "When she come to the building, I see her flirt with Tony. She like him very much. But big trouble if her father know."

Ann told him in greater detail about Elise telling her she would make sure she never passed XCAS—and would never graduate—if her father found out about her and Tony. "That's why Tony shot at me—he was afraid of losing his job and his power. The woman who they scared away by making Lep fix the wiring in her apartment will talk about that, I'm sure. So will the family with little kids whose balcony railing they made him loosen. So will the man whose toilet Lep had to break so that sewage would come out all over his apartment—and Lep had to clean it up. We have the test answers they used to bribe Lep. We have hard evidence and real witnesses—such as you—to prove that the people who get rich from the test use it to threaten and endanger other people—such as me and those people in the building."

She paused, and then said very slowly and distinctly, "All that matters is test scores, to the teachers, the principals, the superintendents. So that it's easy for them to pigeonhole us. What *doesn't* matter is students really learning anything. So . . . do we have a story?"

The phone rang on Mr. Gilroy's desk. He picked

it up quickly. "Yeah? . . . Oh . . . Tell them I'll be right there."

Ann and Lep looked at each other. They carefully kept their faces blank. They didn't want him to see how disappointed they were that he wasn't more interested.

Mr. Gilroy hung up the phone. "Sorry," he said. "What was it you just asked me?"

"I said, we have witnesses and we have hard evidence," Ann reminded him. "So, do we have a story?"

"A story?" he said. "What kind of a story?"

Maybe he hadn't understood after all. "A story about Grath Hull, Mr. Warren's company that publishes the test for the government."

Mr. Gilroy nodded slowly. "Maybe," he said.

"Have you listened to what these kids have told you," Ms. Summers said, rising from her chair and glaring down at the reporter.

"I said 'maybe.' I'll have to investigate myself," Mr. Gilroy said, and pushed the test answers back at Ann and stood up as well. "I've got an important meeting now."

"How did you break your nose, Elise?" her father asked her. "That operation was very expensive, you know. It's going to cost a lot to fix it again."

Elise looked in her hand mirror for the hundredth time, and wiped her tears away with her other hand. Her nose was swollen and twisted to the side. She didn't want to leave the house. She didn't want anybody at school to see her like this. And she especially didn't want Tony to see. Now she couldn't go out with him again until it was fixed. How long would that take?

"Why aren't you answering me, Elise? It's a simple enough question."

She was surprised her father wasn't more sympathetic. She was also angry at herself for not planning a story before he saw her. She didn't want to tell him she had anything to do with the Forrest girl. He wouldn't like her associating with someone so poor and working class, if he even remembered who Forrest was anymore. He would want to know why she had sought Ann out, and of course she couldn't tell him *that*. "I got hit with a volleyball in PE," she said.

"What's the name of the teacher who let that happen?" her father said. "I'll call the school and have her fired. I could sue the school too," he said thoughtfully. "They shouldn't endanger students with rough games like that."

"Don't call the school!" she said quickly. "It was my fault. I wasn't paying attention. I didn't see it coming. Please, just get me an appointment with the plastic surgeon. I can't go back to school until it's fixed."

He sighed. "Nothing like this ever happened to you before," he said. "What was the matter with you? Why weren't you paying attention? What's on your mind these days, anyway? You've been distracted for a week or so."

"Please don't keep badgering her, dear," her mother dared to say. "She must be in a lot of pain. She needs to go to the doctor at least to get some painkillers."

He didn't even bother to answer her. "What's on your mind, Elise? I want to know what's behind all this. You've been acting strange ever since I made the mistake of bringing you to that crummy building. Are you sure it doesn't have anything to do with Tony? I suppose girls find him attractive. If you're thinking about him, I'll have to get rid of him. I know where to find guys like that."

The whole reason she had confronted the Forrest girl was to *prevent* her father from finding out about Tony! Now it was backfiring on her. She wished she had killed her instead of just slapping her and threatening her. She should have *made* her ride in the helicopter and then pushed her out. Henry had been too drunk to notice. She was lucky he hadn't crashed.

"Who's Tony?" Elise said, trying to sound pathetic and innocent.

Her father sighed again—a deeper, more dangerous sigh. "You know damn well who he is!" he snapped. "You called him and interfered with our meeting. I bet that jerk really *did* wink at you. I should probably fire him right now."

"Please, dear," her mother said, unwisely.

"OK, OK, you can call the damn doctor!" her father said angrily. "But I still think there's something suspicious about this whole nose thing. If anything like this happens again you're going to be in deep trouble. And Tony will be too."

On Tuesday morning Mr. Gilroy's paper had a story in the local business section about Elise Warren, daughter of oil and test publishing tycoon Frederick Warren, who owned the Warren Building, the tallest skyscraper in the city. The story said that the daughter of a former worker at a slum building owned by Warren claimed that Elise had threatened to send her to a detention center, and that she'd flunk XCAS if she told anyone Elise had been running around with the building manager of the same slum building. The girl, Ann Forrest, also claimed that the building manager had shot at her to scare her from telling anyone about him and Elise.

In the last paragraph there was very brief mention that a resident of the building claimed the building manager had given him test answers to do illegal things to the apartments of some of the tenants in the building. It mentioned Lep's name, but didn't say what the building manager had asked him to do.

Ann was so disappointed in the story she felt like punching out Gilroy. The story said she and Lep had both "claimed" these things. Gilroy had seen the shooting and he had seen the test answers. Why did he have to say "claim" when he knew they were true? What happened to his investigation?

Of course he was afraid of Warren, who had connections to the federal government.

And to make it even worse, right next to the story was a rebuttal by Warren himself. Gilroy hadn't warned them that he was going to do this. It was just the same as if he had lied to them. Warren said that both of these irresponsible "children" had strong motivations for making problems for his family and his business. He said that Ann Forrest's father had lost his job because of interfering with the building manager's relations with the tenants, who were treated more than fairly.

He said that Lep had no hope of passing XCAS on his own (a test written by highly trained and respected educators) and that he was trying to blame Tony for the test answers he had stolen himself. Ann wanted to punch Gilroy even more when she read that, it made her so furious.

Ann was angry but she was also depressed. Perhaps what her father had said—and what Lep had said at the beginning—was right: People like them could never win against someone like Warren.

Ann took the paper with her so that her father wouldn't see the article right away; people often stole their newspaper from the hallway anyway. But there was going to be big trouble when he inevitably did see it.

Ann's mother left the place so early on Tuesday morning that she didn't have a chance to see the news stories before Ann left home. She was nervous about walking alone to school, so she went a different way again. But nothing happened.

None of the other students seemed to have seen the story. Ann didn't know whether to be relieved or disappointed. She couldn't wait until lunch so that she and Lep could commiserate with each other.

During homeroom, first period, a note was delivered to Ann's homeroom teacher. She nodded to Ann and said without expression, "The principal would like to see you." Ann tried not to be apprehensive, but she couldn't help it when she was admitted to Miss Blight's office and there was a man in there with her, a big fat man in a gray suit. "This is Mr. Mariani, the superintendent of schools," said Miss Blight, the principal. "Ann Forrest. Please sit down, Ann."

Lep was already there, looking miserable.

Now Ann remembered that the superintendent had been in the news last year. He had wanted to make it so that seniors who didn't pass XCAS could still graduate; it would just say on their diploma that they hadn't passed that test. The governor had responded by saying that if the superintendent did that, all the state funding would be taken away from his school district. The superintendent had backed down. Maybe there was a good side to him. But he wouldn't be happy about more XCAS publicity.

"Mr. Mariani was wondering if it was necessary for you to tell that reporter about the personal problems you're having because of your father's involvement in Mr. Warren's business," Miss Blight said.

"The reporter was there when Mr. Warren's hit man shot at me—he saw it with his own eyes, even if he didn't say so," Ann defended herself. "Am I supposed to let these people do terrible things to me and then *not* tell a reporter when I have the chance? He also *saw* the test answers they gave Lep to bribe him to do their dirty work. He left that part out too. He's afraid of Warren." She wanted to add, "And you're afraid of him too," but she was now so worried about the repercussions—more for Lep than herself—that she managed to control herself, barely.

Mr. Mariani and Miss Blight looked at each other without expression, and then Mr. Mariani cleared his throat. "According to the practice results, it looks like we're going to make AYP this year," he began.

"AYP?" Ann asked him, even though she knew what it meant.

"Adequate Yearly Progress," he said. "But now, because of this . . . publicity, they might take us off the list even if the students *do* do better, and we won't get more funding. That's very important, Ann."

"I understand that," Ann said. "But do you really expect me to let them *kill* me so that the school district can get more funding?" She shrugged. "Self-preservation. It's an instinct. I don't want to die."

"We're not asking you to risk your life," Miss Blight said, managing to sound reasonable. "It would just be better if you'd been a little more discreet about it."

"If we lose our funding, every student in the district will be hurt by it," Mr. Mariani added.

She was thinking, for the millionth time, how the test controlled everything and everybody in public education.

"And as for you, Lep," Miss Blight said, frowning. "Well, you have to understand that we can't have it publicly known that one of our students was caught cheating on XCAS. We've arranged for you to be moved back to the juvenile detention center where you were last year. Today."

"What?" Ann shouted, surprising even herself. She sprang to her feet, leaning toward the desk, her hands on her hips. "You can't *do* that! He didn't ask for those test answers. They bribed him with them

to get him to endanger other people in the building! And he's doing better than ever in English now. Just ask Ms. Summers. Ask her!"

"We've heard enough about Ms. Summers already, from other students and their parents. There have been many complaints that she is not preparing her students adequately for XCAS. She is no longer employed by this district, nor will she ever be again." Miss Blight stood up. "And do not speak to me in that tone of voice, young lady," she said, "or you'll be expelled too." She turned back to Lep. "You'd better clean out your locker—the people from the detention center will be here soon to take you back there. Get your things and wait for them outside my office. I'm afraid you won't have a chance to go home first."

"I don't have a home," he said quietly. "My sister looking for new place for our family to live."

Miss Blight ignored that remark—anyone who cheated on XCAS was so criminal that it didn't matter whether his family had a place to live. "You'd better go home yourself, Ann. You're suspended for the rest of the day. This will go on your record. I'd suspend you for longer but I don't want your scores to go down."

Ann knew they were glad to have a reason to get rid of Lep because he'd bring down the school's AYP. And she knew the principal wasn't suspending her for longer for the same reason. "You are both dismissed," Miss Blight said.

"But . . ." Ann said. "But . . ."

"I said, you are both dismissed. If you don't do what I ask, you will *both* be in more serious trouble than you already are." Miss Blight walked over and opened her office door and gestured abruptly for them to leave.

Ann wanted to stay and argue with them not to send Lep back to that place. But she could see from their faces that there was no hope of that. She had probably made things worse by getting angry at them.

The two of them went out to the hall. They put their arms around each other and clung together for a long moment without saying anything. Ann started to cry. This was like a nightmare. Talking to that lying reporter had just made everything a million times worse.

"Oh, Lep, I'm so sorry," she said, gasping, pulling

away from him. "You were right from the beginning. We shouldn't have done anything." She knew that now he had no chance for a better life. And he been struggling so hard for it.

"Ann, I know you try to make things better," he said, his hands still on her shoulders. "You never think it will be like this. I never think that too."

"But what are we going to *do*? You can't go back to that place! And what about your family?"

"Maybe can move to building where Komron work as security. No Tony there. And maybe . . . maybe I can run away before those people come. Go and hide someplace."

"I'll give you all the money I can. I'll keep giving it to you," she said, her nose running now. And she had no tissues.

Lep pulled a wad of toilet paper out of his pocket and wiped her nose. "Don't forget, we have Ms. Summers's number. I know she really on our side, not like reporter. Maybe she think of something."

"Good idea. We can call her as soon as we get out of here. Listen. Come home with me now. Tony won't be following me, it's still just the beginning of the school day. Anyway, what difference does it make anymore? He knows we know each other." She looked at her watch. "The bell's going to ring any minute. We better get out of here fast. Let's get your stuff and go."

Lep's locker was almost completely empty, unlike Ann's, which was crammed with junk. They were heading out the back door just as the bell rang. "This way," Ann said. "We can't go past the principal's office or she might see you." They got away from the school as fast as they could, and started off toward Ann's apartment. "Nobody will be home now," she said. "And if Spencer forgot his phone—he forgets it all the time—you can have it."

"Don't want to take your brother phone."

"You have to. I have to be able to reach you. Everybody will just think he lost it. Let's head over to the other side of that parking lot where we'll be behind all those cars and nobody can see us. Then we can call Ms. Summers."

She got her recorded message. "Hi. It's Ann Forrest. You saw that stupid article. It ruined everything, because of that lying reporter. You got fired. They're trying to make Lep go back to the detention center. I got suspended. Sorry to bother you, but we all need to do something about this. Please call me as soon as you can."

When she put her phone back in her bag she saw her little recorder. She groaned. "My fault *again*! I forgot to play him the tape of Elise threatening me. That would have convinced him. Then the article would have been different."

They started off toward her place again. "No," Lep said. "Don't blame yourself. How he know it really her voice? Wouldn't change anything. He put in what Warren say because he scared, and because reader like to see people saying different thing. More exciting." He laughed bitterly and shook his head. "I don't think safe to ever trust news people."

"You're right about *that*!"

Lep looked curiously around Ann's apartment. It was probably spacious compared to where he lived. Or used to live. To Ann, it seemed smaller and more confining the older she got. "So Tony threw you out?" she asked him. "How did he find out so early?"

"He not. My sister decide herself not stay there. After what I tell her about talking to reporter. Don't want to go to jail school. But don't want to live with my sister when she so mad at me."

"I wonder if my parents would let you stay here for awhile. They might let you sleep on the couch."

He shook his head. "No," he said firmly. "Don't want to make problem for your family. Anyway, if you know where I am, the school find a way to make you tell them, and then they take me to that jail school. I find a place to hide. I live outside in Bangkok after parent die, before my sister bring me here. I can do again. Warm now too."

Ann felt like she was going to start crying again. She was about to say, "It's all my fault," but stopped herself. She'd already said it enough.

She looked in Spencer's room and, in fact, his phone *was* there. She handed it to Lep. "They'll think he lost it. Now I can always talk to you."

He hesitated.

"Lep! You have no choice. I have to be able to

reach you, no matter what. Spencer doesn't need it as much as you do."

He took it reluctantly and put it in his backpack. "Better go now," he said.

"Don't you want something to eat? Don't you want to rest a little? Nobody will be back for hours." Now *she* was the one trying to persuade somebody to stay at her house.

"No. I go now. Parent don't like finding me here." He moved toward the door.

She knew how stubborn he could be. "Wait five minutes. Come with me."

They went into the kitchen and she made him two thick peanut butter and jelly sandwiches and packed them in a strong zipper bag. She knew where her parents kept emergency cash, and gave him two twenties. It took another five minutes for her to convince him to take the money. Then he headed for the door again.

"Can't you at least let me come with you and help you find someplace to—"

"No. Better if I go alone. I told you, if you know where I stay, they will try to make you tell them.

They want to put me in jail again. Safer for you if you don't know."

He wouldn't give in. "I'll call you," she said.

"Thank you for everything," he said. They hugged again, for a long time. And he left.

She brooded and paced the apartment for hours. She had to force herself not to call him immediately. But she knew he needed time to himself.

"Elise," her father said, in a different voice, when he came home from work Tuesday evening. "Elise. Exactly what did you say to the Forrest girl?"

Elise hadn't seen the paper, and neither had her mother. Her mother had already made two appointments for the next day, first with a surgeon, then with a plastic surgeon. While waiting for the appointments they both just watched TV all the time. Elise didn't leave the house. She felt very sorry for herself. She was eating a lot and throwing up even more.

"You don't know how important this is," her father

said. Elise felt a chill. This was his worst voice. This was the quiet voice everyone who knew and worked with him was so terrified of. "Elise. What did you say to the Forrest girl? Exactly."

"What are you talking about?" she whined. "Why do you think I said anything to somebody like that? I don't even know her."

"Elise?" her father said coldly, handing her a page from a newspaper. "He interviewed me last night, but I didn't want to say anything until I could show you this."

Elise started to read. It was difficult to concentrate at first, knowing her father was watching her steadily. But then she saw what the article was about, and she was hooked. She read it with mounting horror. When she put the paper down her father was still staring at her. She couldn't meet his eyes and looked away.

"Why did you tell her that you had anything to do with a juvenile detention center? Why did you tell her that you could make sure she failed XCAS?"

"She's lying. I never did any of that stuff. It's just what you said here." She pointed at his rebuttal.

"She made it all up because her father had to stop working there."

"So how did your nose get broken? I called your school. They haven't played volleyball there for months. They do hockey in the spring."

"I told you, she must have made it all up," Elise insisted hopelessly. She didn't know what else to say.

"Then how does she know so much? How does she know about my connection with the detention center and with XCAS? Why does she believe you went out with Tony?"

"Tony?" her mother said, shocked. "Elise!"

Even her mother was against her now. "I feel sick. I'm going upstairs," Elise said.

"You're staying right here until you tell me absolutely everything that happened. There's nothing that says I have to have your nose fixed. I can easily let you spend the rest of your life with a deformed broken nose. It will get worse too if we don't do anything about it. Which is exactly what I'm going to do if you don't tell me absolutely everything."

Elise broke down. Tears running down her face, she told him everything—about Tony and about the Forrest family seeing them together, about not wanting anybody to find out, about getting Henry drunk so he wouldn't tell, about her confrontation with Ann Forrest and the threats she had to make in hopes of keeping her quiet. Her father watched her impassively the whole time. Her mother's mouth fell open.

"I was trying to protect you!" she insisted. "She knew too much and I wanted to make sure she wouldn't tell anybody. Who would ever think she would do something like *this*?"

"You are very, very lucky the reporter was fair and gave me a chance to tell my side," he said. "Still, I will find ways of punishing you for being so very, very stupid. You will make up for what you have done. And the first thing I'm going to do is cancel your doctors' appointments. For as long as I feel like it. Just so you can feel what it's like to live with a broken nose."

"You can't *do* that!" she wailed. "It still hurts all the time!"

"I can do whatever I want. A daughter who endangers my empire is a gross liability, and she will learn the consequences of her own stupidity. This is only the beginning. And as for Tony, he's gone. Forever. Kaput."

"No!" she wailed, though it hurt to wail. "You didn't!"

"Of course I did. Do you think I want to employ a thirty-year-old man who goes out with my seventeen-year-old daughter behind my back? You'll never see him again. Unless, of course, he finds you and takes revenge on you for ruining his life. I'm rather *expecting* him to do that, as a matter of fact. You'll get no protection from me or from the staff. After what he does, you'll probably be *more* deformed than you are already. And because of what you have done, I won't be able to afford to fix it. And now I'm going out to dinner. I can't stand the sight of you. And as I eat, I will think about more ways of providing you with what you so richly deserve."

Elise sobbed as he walked away. Her mother made no attempt to comfort her.

When Ann's cell phone rang on Tuesday evening she was in her room, avoiding her parents. She tried not to hope too much that it would be Ms. Summers, but it was.

"I don't believe that school," Ms. Summers said. "The principal called me into her office this morning and canned me. She didn't explain. She didn't give me a chance to tell her how much you kids were learning. She hardly even looked at me. She just told me to pack up my things and get out, and that the district would never hire me again, and she would prevent me from working at any other district too." She sighed. "Where's Lep? Is he really back at that detention center?"

"He's hiding out somewhere. He wouldn't tell me where because he's afraid they'll try to get it out of me. But I gave him a cell phone. I can always reach him."

"Well, I have an idea," Ms. Summers said. "It's kind of far-out. But it just might work. Can you both meet me at the Hot Burger on Columbus Avenue, as soon as possible? I don't want to talk about it over the phone. This school district is so much like the federal government they might be tapping my phone."

"We'll be there," Ann said.

When she called Spencer's cell phone, Lep was glad to hear from her. He still wouldn't tell her where he was staying. But when she told him Ms. Summers wanted to meet them, he sounded excited. "You and Ms. Summers the only ones who understand me, who don't think I'm stupid because my English not perfect. I will be there."

They got to Hot Burger at just the same time. She wondered if Lep had been waiting there for her, not going in until she got there. They were so happy to see each other! They hugged for a long moment.

When they went inside, Ms. Summers was seated at a table by herself, in jeans and a T-shirt.

"So what's your idea?" Ann said, as they sat down across from her.

"Every senior has to pass the English XCAS in order to graduate, right?" Ms. Summers said.

Ann shrugged, the question was so obvious. "Yeah?" she said.

"What if every senior in the school refused to take it?" Ms. Summers said.

"I don't understand," Ann said. The question didn't have meaning to her—just the way the idea of life without the Machine didn't have meaning to the people in the story.

"Just what I said," Ms. Summers told her, with a touch of impatience. "What if you organized a protest on testing days, outside the school. And no one took the test. You could carry signs. *That* sure would make a story! I know about these things from when I was an actress."

It was still hard for Ann to comprehend. But now Lep's eyes lit up and he looked excitedly at her, and laughed. "Principal so mad. Super—whatever you say—even *more* mad, crazy mad!" he said gleefully.

"Could you organize something like that, in the next week?" Ms. Summers asked her. "I'd do what I could to help you."

"They'd just flunk everybody," Ann said blankly, still not really comprehending the idea, since testing was so deeply ingrained in the very foundation of education.

"Is there some way you could send an e-mail around to the students, one they could forward to each other? You said they all hate the test. Could you do it in a way that teachers and parents couldn't understand?"

"Well, yeah . . . I could start a text message tree. Texting is harder to trace, and harder for adults to understand." Now Ann was beginning to get the idea, and she started to feel excited herself.

Lep took her hand, right in front of Ms. Summers. "If nobody take test, what can they do?" he said, grinning so mischievously he was on the verge of looking like an imp from a cartoon of hell.

Ms. Summers sat back in her chair and folded her arms over her bosom.

Right there, Ann sent a text message to Randa, Jeff, and Jake. "all senrs boycott XCAS nxt wk. fwd to evrybdy. no adlts."

When they left, Ann said to Lep, "I can't stand to think of you living on the street! You've got to—"

"I find my sister," he said. "I live there. They move to different building. Jail school can't find me there."

She was so happy that she kissed him. It lasted for awhile, right there in front of the Hot Burger.

At home, she left a message to Mr. Gilroy about the boycott next Monday. He hadn't done a very good job with his story in the paper, but he was the only media person she knew.

And when she got to school Wednesday morning it was immediately apparent that her text message had been forwarded all around the school. She was surrounded before she reached the front doors.

A lot of the top students were angry. "Do you expect us not to graduate?"

She had to explain that she had been shot at by

Warren's goon. "Do you think I should keep my mouth shut and let that man keep shooting at me?" Ann told them. "It was in the paper yesterday. The reporter was there when it happened."

"But why this boycott business?"

"It's the only way we have to try to stop them."

People like Randa and Jake, who had more problems with XCAS, were excited. "Do you really think it'll work?" they wanted to know.

"What can they do if nobody takes the test?"

What was very clear was that no one had intercepted the text messages. The teachers didn't seem to know anything about the test boycott. They were drilling the students for the big XCAS next week harder than ever. The teachers' futures, as well as the students', depended on test scores. Or so the teachers still seemed to believe. The fact that no one had told any teacher or administrator about the boycott plans was a measure of just how much the students hated XCAS.

When Ann walked into English the desks were back in rows, the teacher's desk in the front again. An older woman stood behind the desk, very thin, with gray hair, wearing a tweed pantsuit.

After the buzzer the new teacher shook the sheaf of papers in her hand. "The last substitute seems to have been irresponsible and let you down," she said, not introducing herself. "We'll have to work very hard for the next few days to get you back on track before XCAS next week." She walked around the desk and came down the aisles, passing out photocopied papers, with the Replico logo at the bottom. "You have ten minutes to study this test preparation paragraph and then we're having a quiz."

No more reading real stories. No more interesting class discussions, no more learning things that gave them insights into real life. Test preparation, like Mr. Wells. Ann didn't understand the new paragraph at all, which was about battle tactics in a war between jet fighter planes. After the new teacher collected the test papers, she handed them more paragraphs to read at home tonight. "And there'll be two more quizzes tomorrow," she said. "Concentrate as hard as you can, for your own sakes. You poor kids need a chance to catch up."

"'Poor kids' is right," Ann muttered to Randa when they were outside the room after class. "But we'll get them for this."

At lunch the next day more people sat with Ann than ever before, including a lot of very important students, such as the president of the student council. The whole table was talking about Ms. Summers in hushed voices so no teacher would hear. Those who had been in her classes told the other ones what it was like. "Can you believe an English class that was actually *interesting*, maybe even *fun*?" one of the boys said. "It was cool finding out what technology they had in 1909."

"It used to be like that all the time, or so people tell me," Ann said. "And maybe it'll be like that again some day, if we can depend on everybody."

"I still don't know if this boycott thing is worth risking flunking," one of the smartest boys said.

"Think of the kids who do well in their classes but can't pass XCAS," Ann said. "They'll never get into college. You might not know what their lives are going to be like, but I do. And it isn't pretty."

On Friday Ann called Lep and told him that they were having a meeting of the boycott organizers at her friend Jake's house on Saturday night. "Not a party, a meeting. Come over to my house at five and we'll get a ride."

"But . . ."

"You can't avoid this, Lep. It'll be fine. We need somebody from every homeroom to organize this. We need you. You won't get caught. Nobody has to know where you live now."

He got there early and had to walk around the block before he rang the bell. He wasn't used to having all this free time, and a lot of things took less time than he expected. When he was working for Tony all the time he had often been late. Ann came down right away with her father. It was odd to see him. It brought back all the bad old feelings of being Tony's slave at Grand Diamond.

Her father was very nice to him, beaming as he shook his hand; he seemed more relaxed than when he had worked at Grand Diamond. "Good to see you, Lep," he said. "That must have been very difficult to be honest about the test answers. It might be hard at first, but in the long run it will probably do a lot of good to expose them like that." At first Lep was pleased, but then he understood that of course that's what Mr. Forrest would say; Tony had always hated him, and now Mr. Forrest was surely fired. *Som nam na* meant "serves you right" in Thai—though it was much dirtier and nastier than in English.

"There's Jeff," Ann said. "His parents let him have the car tonight. Let's go."

Lep and Ann sat in back, and Randa sat in front with Jeff. The three Americans were talking so fast that Lep could barely understand them. The whole meeting was probably going to be like that. Lep stopped listening and looked out the window. He had never been in a neighborhood like this. The houses were big, and far apart from each other, and surrounded by green lawns. But no one was growing vegetables or rice; no one had chickens or cows. So what was all that land for, anyway?

Lep was also puzzled by the spaciousness of Jake's house. It seemed that Jake and his parents were the only people who lived there. So what did they need all these rooms for? And they were putting on an addition. How much room did they need? Would they ever be satisfied? The families Lep had known in Thailand all lived in one room.

He was glad that Ms. Summers was at the meeting. Because she was there, the meeting was better than Lep had expected. She was in charge and made sure that the students spoke one at a time, and slowly, not loudly, so it was easier for Lep to understand.

They had to decide how the boycott was going to begin. Should they go into school at all on Monday, or just start marching and demonstrating before school started? If they started before school, they'd have to get there incredibly early. It would also be more difficult to organize; people might just be aimlessly milling around. If they went to homeroom first, they'd all be organized and in place at the same time. Then, after first period, instead of going to the big green testing room, they'd just walk out the school doors. Jake had a big van. They could put the signs in there, he could park nearby, and they could just pick up the signs after they left the school.

When they thought about how the teachers and administrators would react to that, they got even more excited. They all started talking at once, and laughing, and Ms. Summers had to focus them again.

"Here's the most important thing," she said. "Everything has to be really orderly and controlled, or we won't be able to pull this off at all. I *cannot* emphasize that enough! You don't want to act like a mob; you have to be responsible, serious adults." Some of the kids looked a little downcast at that, and Ms. Summers added, "This is not a party. We're not doing this for the fun of it. We're doing it to make a very important statement. And to try to make a change. This is serious." She glared around at everyone in the room. There wasn't a sound. She lowered her voice and added, "Now text that to everyone you know. You hear me? You going to do that?"

They all nodded. Lep hoped they would do it.

Lep had already known Ms. Summers was on their side—the boycott was her idea. But he still wondered why she was making this sacrifice, why she was publicly joining their cause. She would never get any other teaching job anywhere else. Her motivation was confusing, and Lep wished he knew the answer.

Ann had told Lep that Jake had little hope

of passing XCAS, in math as well as English. That's why his parents were benevolent hosts to this meeting. Jake's father owned some kind of advertising company and had provided them with heavy sheets of cardboard to make signs with. After the formal part of the meeting was over the kids went down to the family room on the lower floor and began trying to figure out what to say on the posters. The main idea was to make fun of the XCAS slogans.

"No Child Left Behind" was the most important phony slogan for XCAS—the main reason that phrase was so phony was that XCAS not only left kids, it got rid of them. But it was taking much more thought and argument than they had expected to come up with something apt with those letters: NCLB.

"New Curriculum Lets Us Bloom" sounded clumsy, and didn't really say anything: It could be *any* new curriculum, after all, just as bad as the old one. Try as they might, none of the smartest kids there could think of anything useful at all. The whole room sank into a gloomy silence. How could they have a boycott and a demonstration without posters?

Then Lep had an idea. "What if they don't mean anything?" he said.

"What's that supposed to mean?" a tall boy asked.

"That guy was against the boycott from the beginning," Ann whispered. "Go ahead, Lep."

"Well, if they were just all . . . non . . . non . . ." He turned to Ann and Ms. Summers.

"Nonsense!" Ann said, clapping her hands with a little jump. "If we had the original slogan, and then have it equal something that didn't mean anything at all, it would show how it never meant anything in the first place! Like . . . maybe . . . 'No Child Left Behind' equals . . . uh . . . 'Never Cripple Limited Bambis!'"

Some of the kids looked totally confused. Others actually laughed.

"Not 'limited,'" Lep said, thinking of Limited English Proficiency. "Maybe . . . 'Never Cripple Lollipop Bambis!'"

Everybody laughed at that one.

"Right on, Lep and Ann!" Ms. Summers said. "If people who are watching this demonstration laugh, if they see some humor in it, that will help to get them on our side."

Then the kids became inspired. "Adequate Yearly Progress" turned into "Antagonize Your Pantyhose." "Department of Education" was "Death of Eccentricity." "Limited English Proficiency" became "Laminate Everyone's Poo." (Ms. Summers was a bit doubtful about that one, but she was overruled—after all, "poo" was just a baby word.)

The kids were having so much fun now, and so motivated, that they no longer needed supervision. Ms. Summer and Ann and Lep sat down in a corner of the room. "Well, Lep. It seems as though you've become one of the organizers," Ms. Summers said.

Ann nodded in a agreement, grinning.

And Lep thought, *If I'm one of the organizers, maybe I can ask a question that might be a little rude.* He got sick of being polite all the time. "Ms. Summers," he said. "We all think what you doing is real great—never happen without you. But what

I don't see"—Ann shot him a warning glance, but he ignored it—"I don't see what it doing for *you.* You never get teaching job after this. You just doing to *help*? But why you care?"

"*Lep!*" Ann hissed at him.

Ms. Summers relaxed back in her chair and crossed her legs. "Of course I hate XCAS and I hate seeing it take away the best learning years of your lives. I hate seeing what it does to people who need more help, like you, Lep, and like other kids who have special needs for other reasons—the ones who are really left behind. It slows the bright kids down too. I also see how it ruins the teachers' lives."

She sighed and smiled, her large eyes roaming over the ceiling. "And do you think, as a former actress, I won't *like* it if this gets on TV? And if it goes network? It probably will, you know. What harm is that going to do *me*? Sure, I can't teach anymore—and I know I'm a darn good teacher. But in my heart, I'm an actress. And I always was. Nothing's going to bother me if it leads back in that direction. Too old for the ingenues. Of course." She sat forward and rubbed her hands. "But character parts. That's something you can really dig your teeth into." And she smiled in a kind of reverie.

Ann and Lep met each other's eyes. If Ms. Summers was in this at least partly for herself, then they could really believe that she would never let them down, no matter what.

Right?

Monday morning, the first day of XCAS.
The second buzzer rang and they all settled down
in homeroom, trying to act as normal as possible.
Ann wasn't used to situations like this. She felt that
her whole body was ringing, sending out vibrations
that everybody could hear. She kept looking around
surreptitiously to see if anybody noticed, especially
the teachers, but nobody seemed to. The students
were just acting unusually alert, which was normal
for a testing day.

Lep, hiding outside the school, was more
accustomed than Ann to being in tense situations.
He was used to being yelled at by Tony; he was used

to being out on an eighth-floor balcony loosening the screws so that at any minute the railing might fall off; he was used to dealing with dangerous and unpredictable electric wiring. He remembered when he had first entered this country, how calm and imperturbable he had to be when the tough immigration guards asked him nasty questions about drugs and violence and went through every item in his small suitcase—not that there were many items. He knew how to ignore their hostile glares when they finally, begrudgingly, let him through.

Of course, Ann didn't know what all the other homeroom teachers were saying, but it had to be pretty much the same thing: "No need to be nervous . . . Just concentrate hard . . . Don't let your mind wander . . . You are all well prepared . . . there will be silent breaks with snacks . . . Your test-practice went better than ever this year, everyone is sure we will make AYP." They also read from a test booklet. "This test is untimed. You will have until the end of the day to finish it. The test will consist of multiple choice, short answer, and long answer. Read every question three times. Read all parts of the question and label your answers for the short and long answers. Any form of talking or any eye contact with another student will be considered cheating and will result in your test being taken away. You will be given a zero. Good luck," and blah, blah, blah. The same things they always said before every big XCAS. But this one was bigger than every other. This one determined whether they would graduate, and that determined the rest of their lives.

And every student in the school could feel it in the teachers: *They* were the ones who were really tense. Their positions, their salaries, even their jobs depended on how the students were going to do today. Knowing this gave the students a kind of power, a power they had never felt before, a power over the teachers, over the school, over the entire establishment. The *students* had the power to send it all toppling today, *without* violence, *without* the primitive security measures and shackles the administration had to use to keep the students under control. The students were now in a position to be above all that.

The second buzzer shrilled. Homeroom was over.

As usual, the students all stood up at once. As usual, they took their books and put them in their lockers—they never brought their books to the green testing room on XCAS days. Ann thought of the test booklets and the sharpened number two pencils neatly arranged on the testing tables. The poor lonely little pencils and booklets expecting to be used, expecting to be so important. How disappointing for them!

What a weird thought! She shook her head to get rid of it. She was going to have to be completely down-to-earth today.

The moment the lockers were closed and locked, everything changed. Every senior in the school turned and headed for the front doors.

The first to notice were the other students. They were confused. The normally orderly procession in the hallways was not normal and orderly today. The seniors weren't following the pattern. What was going on? What were the underclassmen supposed to do?

Next, curity caught on. When curity saw that all the seniors were heading for the front doors, they lined up across them. Curity couldn't figure it out, because of course all the students knew that closed-circuit cameras were trained on both the inside and the outside of the doors, photographing every person who went either way. The cameras—which did not have to be paid a salary—were supposed to keep the students in order; that's why there weren't enough physical bodies of the curity police to actually control the student body as a whole. The students knew this, of course; it was part of their plan. Some of them were stopped, which was to be expected. The ones curity could not stop just kept right on going, out through the front doors.

Out toward the waiting TV camera. This time, Gilroy seemed to have come through.

The forty curity guards stopped a pathetic few of the five hundred and thirty seniors. The first ones through ran for Jake's van, parked right across the street from the school. It had been a sacrifice for Jake, who was naturally lazy, to get up early enough to get this place, but a friend of his who was more alert had slept over the night before to make sure Jake got up on time.

Once the freshmen, sophomores, and juniors, from the first floor and the upper floors, saw the

TV camera and the posters, knowing this was senior XCAS day, they immediately understood. They hated XCAS too, of course, and so they headed for the front doors, ignoring the orders of their teachers, ignoring the bells the teachers rang in the office, which were ignored there as well.

With the other students joining in, curity was completely overwhelmed. Almost the entire student body was headed outside now, into a day of bright sunshine and cool breezes. Curity couldn't call for reinforcements from other schools—all the other schools were also understaffed for curity, because curity required human beings who had to be paid; the other schools couldn't manage without them.

The various teachers reacted in their own individual ways. After all, their jobs were at stake. If Wells had been there he would have been running around and screaming. But he wasn't there. He had been carried away on a stretcher.

Miss Blight, the principal, sat in her office, her face pale as death, speaking in controlled tones through the public address system. Bells shrilled around her but she ignored them. "Students," she said in a steady, unwavering, expressionless voice. "This is unheard of. Anyone who does not return to the school immediately and proceed directly to the testing room will automatically fail XCAS and never graduate. Do you hear me? Anyone who does not return to the school immediately and proceed directly to the testing room will automatically fail XCAS and never graduate. Anyone who does not return to the school immediately and proceed directly to the testing room . . ." Over and over again Miss Blight repeated her unheard words. She would keep repeating them for some time to come.

Female and male teachers tried to reinforce curity at the front doors. Yes, they managed to push some of the students inside. But now that the entire student body had joined the boycott, though only the seniors were to be tested today, the flood of students was impossible to push back. Whenever one was thrust inside, three more came pouring through.

There was a detainment room. It held ten students. The problem was, the regular teachers weren't used to wrestling with struggling students, especially students who had a purpose that was not simply making trouble; and curity, who did have some fighting techniques, were now trapped at the front doors. The detainment room remained empty. No student would have missed being outside for the world.

Ann and Lep found each other quickly. They had decided not to carry posters. They hurried for Mr. Gilroy, who was standing behind the camera. A familiar TV reporter was standing in front of the camera, waiting. "Good job," Mr. Gilroy said. "This is just our station. All the others will be here momentarily."

"But why did you believe we could really pull this off?" Ann asked.

"I was impressed by you both when you came to my office. If anybody could do this, you two could."

"But you didn't help us very much with that newspaper story—especially by putting in what Warren said."

He shrugged. "Disagreements make good copy. The managing editor made me do it. That issue sold a lot of papers." He looked across at the students, his brow slightly furrowed. "We haven't started shooting yet. They'll be orderly, won't they?"

"Those were the instructions," Ann said. It was the first time Lep had heard her sounding nervous, except for when Tony had shot at her. Lep, who was more experienced in the world, wasn't nervous at all.

"Here." Mr. Gilroy handed Ann a megaphone. "If you have any doubts, use this."

Ann did have doubts. Only a few of the students had posters, holding them straight and high. The rest were just milling around, as if this were a sort of party. She saw a group of kids lighting cigarettes. That was all wrong; it would ruin everything. They had talked about that Saturday night. The big mistake was that they had made no definite plan about how to *maintain* order, like an army would have. They *had* to be brought under control!

Ann had always prided herself on being able to act however she wanted in any situation. But when she cleared her throat through the megaphone thing, it sounded like a cough. Nobody paid attention. They just milled around. It was great that the underclassmen had joined, but it didn't help that they had not heard

Ms. Summers's pep talk Saturday night or received any text messages about it: keeping in order, marching in a line, acting like adults. Ann sighed. She felt herself blushing. She lifted the megaphone to try again.

And then, on the street to the right of the statue of the man on the horse, sat Tony. Not on the Replico bike, no Replico helmet. He was on the bike that he had used when he shot at her. A chill went through her. What was he doing here? He still hated her! He was out to ruin this thing. And now he had seen her and Lep together. Did he have a gun? Her voice dried in her throat.

She turned to Lep. He was looking at Tony too, his face expressionless. "Tony?" Mr. Gilroy said softly. "The man who shot at you?"

Suddenly Ann felt hopeless. The whole thing, which had seemed so promising, was falling apart.

"Please?" Lep said politely, and took the megaphone from her limp hand.

What he had said to the group of students Saturday night seemed to have worked. Why not try again, now that Ann was in trouble? The principal might call the people from the detention center, but he didn't think they would forcibly drag him away in front of the TV camera. He turned to Mr. Gilroy. "Can you make it very loud?"

"It's plenty loud enough."

Lep put it to his lips. "You want to be on TV?" he yelled into it.

The students were startled, silent for a moment. Then they all yelled together, "Yeah!"

"Then walk in straight line! Like you see people on TV! Like adult! Find homeroom and walk together. Even, straight line! If don't do that, cops come and take you all away. All will lost! Find homeroom. Walk in straight line. Now!" He paused. "And put out cigarette!"

Lep held the megaphone while they watched. Some students shot him hostile glances, especially kids in lower classes. Who was this jerk to be telling them what to do? Students wandered around in a confused manner. Nothing seemed to be getting any better. He forced himself not to look over to see Tony's expression. "Jeff!" Lep barked into the megaphone. "Randa! Tall boy who against boycott at beginning! Do something. Organize! Or cops will come!"

A lot of the kids were still mumbling in resentment that *he* should be giving *them* orders. But what else could he do? What else *was* there to do?

One by one, he caught sight of the three kids he had singled out. They were all popular and knew a lot of people. They were moving purposefully through the crowd now, pushing kids into order. Ann, having given up on being the leader—leaving it to Lep!— went and joined them.

And then, like a miracle, seemingly out of nowhere, Ms. Summers appeared beside him. She was wearing more glossy makeup than he had ever seen on her, and a red silk brocade jacket and black skirt that looked great on her. "You're doing a super job, Lep. And I'm not one bit surprised," she said, with a smile. "But I think we may need just a *tad* more experience here." She pulled the megaphone out of his hand. "Camera on me?" she said sweetly to Gilroy.

"Yes, *ma'am*!" he said, and nodded at the camera-man, who swiveled the camera away from the reporter and focused right in on Ms. Summers. The red light went on.

"Listen up, kids!" she yelled, smiling. "Lep is right! If you want XCAS to control you for the rest of your lives, if you want corrupt big business to determine your futures, then go on and keep right on doing what you're doing. First thing you know the cops'll end this whole thing for sure. All your planning will fizzle and that'll be the end of it!

"But if you want to beat the test for good, do what Lep here's telling you. Homeroom kids who were at Jake's the other night, raise your hands. Other homeroom kids find yourselves. Find your homerooms and march straight. Fast! You can do it and you better do it if you know what's good for you and every student in this country. *Do it now!*"

She gestured at Gilroy and he had the camera turn toward the students.

The students' faces hardened. A kind of determination came over them. It was amazing how quickly the seniors gathered in homeroom groups. Once that had happened, it seemed easier for the others. They hurried. Ms. Summers kept checking her watch and showing it to Lep. In only five minutes the students had come to order. It was not one big circle. There were too many of them for that in the cement area in front of the school. Instead there were circles within circles, the seniors in the outside circles, and forming around the statue of the man on the horse.

Ms. Summers held out the megaphone to Lep. "I'll have plenty of airtime later. You take this one. You've earned it."

Lens on Lep. "Okay, *move!*" Lep said, feeling self-conscious for the first time and doing his best to hide it. "Stay in line. Do not push! Think about never having XCAS again. That keep you going!" And he raised and shook the fist that wasn't holding the megaphone.

And then, to his total shock, he saw Tony raise his fist and shake it too, in what could only be complete agreement.

But why should he be shocked? OK, Tony hated Ann. But now, having been fired by Warren, he must hate Warren more. And what was happening here could only be very, very bad for Mr. Warren.

That gave Lep the courage to add, "Teachers

too! Come and march. XCAS bad for you as for us. Teachers welcome too!"

And then—how had it happened?—he saw that he was talking to three cameras instead of one. The cameras swiveled around to show the crowd.

A moment later Gilroy signaled to his reporter, pointing to a piece of paper. The reporter nodded. He was as sprucely dressed as Mr. Warren, though a lot taller and more handsome. He beckoned for Lep to come and stand in front of the camera. Gilroy took the megaphone away from him and gave him a gentle shove. And there he was standing next to the reporter, not knowing whether to look at him, or into the lens.

283

"This young man's name is Lep, and he's from Thailand," the reporter said to the camera, and turned and smiled at Lep. "Lep, you seem to be one of the organizers of this test boycott and demonstration. I have many questions to ask you and the other organizer, Ann Forrest. But before we get to the bottom of this, I'm sure our audience has some questions about the strange words on the posters some of the demonstrators are carrying. For instance, to start with you. Can you tell me about the poster that has the letters 'LEP' on it?"

Lep felt shyer than he ever had in his life. He also knew that this might be the most important thing he had ever done in his life. He had to *taeh!* the shyness away.

"You can see on sign. In Thai language, 'lep' mean 'fingernail,' my nickname. In XCAS, 'LEP' mean 'Limited English Proficiency.'" He hoped very much he did not pronounce that wrong! "We want to show on sign that is stupid word. Who can say how is limited? Everybody different! We want to make another word for sign. But nobody know what. So . . . er . . . somebody . . . somebody have idea . . ."

Off camera, Gilroy nudged the reporter. "Could that somebody have been *you*, Lep?"

Lep sighed. "I have idea make new meaning crazy, not mean anything, just like test word don't mean anything. So that why we think of 'LEP' mean 'Laminate Everyone Poo.'" Even though Lep couldn't see his face blushing, he could *feel* the blood going into his face.

"A little humorous too?" the reporter said, chuckling.

Lep shrugged. "Never can hurt to be funny."

"How about some of the other signs?" The other cameras were crowding around him, more than three now.

Lep was beginning to relax into this. "Most important one, 'No Child Left Behind.' The people who make test, they say that is meaning of whole test. But they *wrong*!" He hit his left hand with his right fist. "XCAS leave many, many behind. XCAS leave me behind, because I come from another country and my English not perfect. XCAS leave behind any student who come from home where parent do not read, or any home where too many kid to have enough food. XCAS give no chance to learn anything can use in real life. XCAS only teach how to pass XCAS, like . . . like a circle that go nowhere. 'No Child Left Behind' a *lie!* It mean *nothing*! So we want to show it mean nothing. That why we have sign that say 'NCLB' mean 'Never Cripple Lollipop Bambi.' So that—"

He was interrupted by the laughter of the reporter and the camera crew—and he could only hope the TV audience too. The audience must be pretty large, with all these stations here now.

Next he explained about AYP, Adequate Yearly Progress. "Every year, every school judged on getting better XCAS score," he said. "If students get higher score, school get more money. If student get lower score, school get less money, and teachers get in trouble, maybe even lose job. Doesn't matter if students learn something *real* like in Ms. Summers's class." He gestured at her, the cameras swung toward her, and she flashed a brilliant smile.

Lep saw that Ann was standing beside her, now that the crowd had become orderly. "Ann, please, come and help me," Lep pleaded with her, and Ann joined him, proud and smiling.

"You don't need help, Lep, you're doing great on your own," she said to him conversationally, in front of the cameras. She had regained her nerve.

"He's right," she said to the cameras. "How can you measure real learning with a stupid quiz? So instead of 'Adequate Yearly Progress,' we decided that 'AYP' should mean 'Antagonize Your Pantyhose.'" Again, they were interrupted by laughter.

While the others were laughing, Ann glanced over at the demonstrators again. "Uh oh," she said, and nudged Lep in the ribs, pointing out Mr. Wells, walking with a cane toward the circles of students.

"What he doing here?" Lep whispered.

"He's going to try to stop it now."

"How can he?" Lep said. "He too weak. Need help." And right in front of the camera, Lep ran over and took Wells's arm, and helped him toward the circles of students. And Wells didn't try to stop it. He got in line and started walking along with the students. Another student took his arm so Lep could go back to the camera.

Ann was whispering fiercely to the reporter and Gilroy. Gilroy flipped the power back to the reporter's mike. "That's Mr. Wells, a former teacher who always taught to the test. Now he's joined the student protest. The test is hard on the teachers too."

They could see Miss Blight, looking palely out of her office window as, one by one, twelve teachers joined the march. Now Miss Blight wouldn't get the $20,000 bonus she would have gotten if the school had made AYP. Ann fed the marching teachers' names to the reporter, and all the other reporters picked them up. "This will go nationwide, for sure!" Gilroy kept saying, barely able to keep his excitement under control. He, of course, would receive all the credit for getting this story, growing bigger by the minute, off the ground.

"The governor's office was contacted about this protest. 'No comment' was their response," the reporter told the audience.

"The governor must be terrified of the president," Gilroy wryly murmured.

And then Tony was casually strolling over. Ann felt the old chill again, but she stood her ground. There really *was* nothing he could do now in front of all these newsmen. There was also something different about him today that made her less afraid.

The first thing he did was to reach out and shake Lep's hand. Then he chuckled benignly and shook his head. "Man," he said, "if I'd tried as hard as I damn could to get that creep Warren where it would hurt, I couldn't've come up with anything halfway as good as *this*!" He bent over with his hands on his knees, laughing.

He turned to Ann. "Yeah, OK, you gave me a lotta trouble, girl, when I was his man. But I ain't his man no longer. And even though it kinda hurts me to say this, I gotta tell you that even back then, I felt a kind of respect for you. How many chicks woulda stood up to somebody like me the way you did?"

Ann and Lep didn't know what to say. Gilroy did. "That whole side of the story, Warren's side, isn't being covered here." He gestured over at the still well-organized students. "*That's* this afternoon's story. I don't want to leave Warren out of this. He's just too big and slimy not to cause a huge amount of attention. So here's my idea. We have a special press conference with the four of you, Ann, Lep, Ms. Summers, and Tony. We have it at dinnertime today, when the story is still fresh and everybody can watch it. And we'll repeat it a number of times. We don't want little Mr. Warren left out. That wouldn't be fair to him now, would it? What do the four of you think about that?"

Ann, Lep, Ms. Summers, and Tony all looked at each other. And they smiled in a way none of them had ever smiled before.

25

The press conference was taped. Ann and Lep watched it afterward at Ann's house, with all of Ann's family. How many millions of other people were watching it all across the country?

Because of the studio's excellent makeup artist, all four of them looked stunning. Ann's hair seemed blonder and shinier than ever, her cheeks glowed, her blue, blue eyes sparkled. The body-fitting dark blue velvet dress provided by the studio brought out her eye color even more.

Lep's tawny skin was emphasized with very subtle peachlike tones, which also enhanced the red of his lips without having to use any lipstick. On TV his eyes seemed larger and more expressive than ever, and because of the nature of the TV picture he did not seem as thin as he did in real life. As usual, his proud posture gave him a special alertness. Of course he wore the Replico T-shirt, which was altered slightly by the studio wardrobe so that it did not hang quite so loosely on him. You could see that he had muscles.

Ms. Summers wore the same elegant outfit she had worn at the boycott. She was the only one who knew how to do her own makeup so that her face looked riveting and also warm on the TV screen.

It was decided that Tony looked best in the black clothes he wore habitually anyway. The black, in contrast to his pale skin and white-blond hair and faintly pinkish eyes, gave the odd impression that he was a creature from somewhere in between a Poe story and a bunny rabbit. It was the perfect look for what he had to tell.

Ann, Lep, and Ms. Summers answered reporters' questions first. Because this was a nationwide broadcast, the stories were covered as thoroughly as necessary. Bribing Lep with test answers to do illegal things was corroborated by Tony. The recording Ann made of Elise Warren threatening that Ann would go to detention and flunk XCAS was broadcast to everyone in the auditorium, and was discussed in detail.

Ms. Summers talked about teaching Ann and Lep's English class, and other classes at the school, for several weeks. "I've been away from teaching for awhile, but since all of this happened, I've looked extensively into the XCAS test, and its effect on education as a whole. If it were merely one factor out of many in a student's profile, then it would not be so insidious and damaging. But now the test has become everything. Students' entire futures are determined by it. It prevents intelligent students like Lep from graduating and moving on to a better position in life. It is so powerful that it affects every level of the educational process. Teachers are rated on the basis of their students' test scores. I know from Mr. Wells's notes—he is the teacher I was substituting for—that he wanted Lep to be moved out of his classroom because Lep's test scores would bring down the average. But after his heart attack he changed his mind, and joined the student boycott."

Then the reporters turned to Tony.

He started working for Mr. Warren nine years ago, when he was twenty-one, when Warren was just building Grand Diamond. Back then, Tony had been locked up in the same detention center as Lep would be because of the special questions on XCAS—psychological profiling questions to pinpoint potential terrorists and criminals. It was there, in the adult lockup, that Warren's middleman had found Tony, and many other young people who were adept at making money just outside the law. People like that were what Warren needed in many of his businesses.

Certainly Warren had no plans to build anything that was up to any kind of code for the poor tenants he had in mind. He was already rich enough to pay off any inspectors. The building was constructed as cheaply as possible; every corner was cut. This from a man who was a captain of industry, and who was already amassing more wealth as publisher of the all-important XCAS.

Tony kept his eye on the architect when he made the plans, to be sure no expensive (safe, solid) materials were used. He kept an eye on the builders to be sure they mixed as much sand into the cement as possible. Warren's middleman made sure that Tony was deeply involved in the corruption from the very beginning. Warren wanted to make sure Tony was trapped and could never get out.

The middleman told Tony the plan for the building. Mostly immigrants would live there— immigrants who did not have the proper papers to find other, safer apartments. For this favor, Mr. Warren charged them higher rents than similar apartments in the same neighborhood. The tenants had no choice if they wanted to stay in this country.

Tony's duties: ignore tenants with valid complaints for as long as possible. And for those tenants who would not let up, get the poor immigrant boy, Lep, to fix their apartments to be even less safe. Bribe him with test answers. Warren knew that the penalty for cheating on the test was immediate, permanent expulsion from school. Lep would never say a word to anyone.

"Warren was very secretive, of course," Tony said. "His mistake was not to realize that I knew other people who worked in his oil and publishing businesses, because they had been at the detention center with me. Lep wasn't the only person who was bribed with test answers so that Warren wouldn't get his own hands dirty. He didn't know that I heard certain phone conversations, and had access to certain papers. The connection between his publishing company, Grath Hull, and the federal government, is very close. People often were promoted from Grath Hull to positions in the administration. The government knew what Warren was doing, and tacitly accepted it." He smiled thinly. "They will not be happy now."

After that, there were many questions that further exposed in detail Mr. Warren's shady dealings in all his businesses. The four panelists kept their expressions very serious. Not until the cameras stopped running and all the reporters had left did they start joking and laughing with each other. It feels very good to win against someone so much more powerful than you.

The network press conference blasted across the entire country. In combination with the hugely covered test boycott at their school—in which many teachers had participated—it did just about all that was necessary to make it imperative to rewrite the federal administration's current educational policy.

It was testing week all over the country. The boycott at Ann and Lep's school was only the first of many. "No more XCAS" was the phrase of the hour. So few students took the test that it had to be discredited, for that year at least.

Warren's publishing contract with the government was canceled. His other businesses began to fail as well, because of all the bad publicity. He had to sell his tower, his house, his helicopters, and many other things.

They patched up Elise's nose, but she couldn't live down the scandal about her father's business practices. She became a recluse, and her kitchen sink was always full of dirty dishes.

After doing time for what he had done to Ann, Tony received many offers of film contracts to play monster roles in horror movies. He got rich in Hollywood.

Ms. Summers, because of her commanding

performance on TV during the boycott and her previous acting experience, received a TV contract to be host of her own talk show.

Colleges all over the country sent Ann acceptance notices.

Lep, because of his tremendous communication skills and ability to control groups, was invited to attend Harvard with a full scholarship. Ann, who could go to school anywhere, went with him.

And after that, they were never apart for very long at all.

ABOUT THE AUTHOR

William Sleator is considered a master of science fiction and thrillers for middle-grade readers and young adults. R. L. Stine calls Sleator "one of my favorite young adult writers," and *Publishers Weekly* calls his work "gleefully icky." Sleator divides his time between homes in Boston and rural Thailand.

THIS BOOK WAS ART DIRECTED
by Chad W. Beckerman. The text is set in
12-point Adobe Garamond, a typeface that
is based on those created in the sixteenth
century by Claude Garamond. Garamond
modeled his typefaces on those created by
Venetian printers at the end of the fifteenth
century. The modern version used in this
book was designed by Robert Slimbach,
who studied Garamond's historic typefaces
at the Plantin Moretus Museum in Antwerp,
Belgium.